THE BLOOD OF MONSTERS

HER CURSED PROTECTORS

THE BLOOD OF MONSTERS

OF

MONSTERS

HER CURSED PROTECTORS BOOK 1

MIA HARTSON

ISBN: 978-0-6457298-0-1

First printing edition 2023 in United States

Cover design by Trif Book Design

Copyedited by Lyss Em Editing

Mia Hartson

PO BOX 1052, Golden Grove Village, SA 5125

www.miahartson.com

For anyone who needs an escape, a laugh, and a new obsession.

I hope you enjoy the ride.

Mia x

CHAPTER 1

~ Raine ~

Sweat clung to my skin as I stared at the target, a crudely forged blade in my hand. Seconds. That was all I allowed myself to make sure the aim was right, and then the knife was slicing through the air, spinning until it landed with a *thuck*, burying into the tree trunk I'd selected.

Launching forward, I pulled more blades from my leather pockets as I sprinted in a circle, the wind tugging at my long ponytail. More thuds sounded as my knives sank into the other trees lining the clearing—my makeshift monsters, though I knew they were nothing like the real beings.

I was panting by the time I reached into my last pocket and discovered it was empty. Coming to a halt, I forced my breathing to calm and inspected where my blades had landed. I imagined the steel protruded from real monster flesh, but it was hard when I'd never actually *seen* one of the

Katakin. *Head. Chest. Neck. Arm. And...* I tilted my head to the side, trying to decide on the position of the lowest blade. "Groin," I finally muttered to myself with a smirk. I couldn't be sure that stabbing male monsters in the groin would have the same effect as it would on a man, but either way, I was betting it would hurt like a bitch. *Perfect.*

Striding over, I collected my blades for the dozenth time and stared up at the sky. *Fuck.* I'd been out for too long. Pink had begun to stain the blue, the colors melding above my head. *Time's up, Raine. Get your ass moving.* The Night of the Offering was here, and monsters didn't wait. I took off at a sprint through the trees.

· · · · ● · ● · · ·

Chief Shaasi stood in the middle of the clearing, firelight from her bamboo torch flickering on her skeletal face. My gaze swept across the area, and I continued forward, relieved that the last shadows of twilight were only just starting to disappear from the trees and the clearing was still empty of monsters.

Adding on to the end of the long line of villagers that stretched from one side of the clearing to the other, I ignored Chief Shaasi's glare. I knew why she was cranky, but really, I was chuffed. For a moment there, I hadn't thought I would make it. I'd barely had enough time to race back to my cottage, wipe off the sweat, change, and then I'd run here, twigs scratching my bare feet and fire burning in my lungs.

Pulling my hair from its ponytail, I hastily combed my fingers through my long dark waves, only to have one of my fingers get caught in a knot. Ripping through the knot, I forced the hair to loosen, pulling out a few strands in the process. My eyes began to water, but I blinked the pain away.

A low snicker sounded from someone further along the line, but I didn't bother to see who it had come from.

My attention went back to Chief Shaasi as she raised her wrinkled chin and began to speak, her shrill voice grating against my ears. "Daughters of the Goddess, Falia, ten years have passed, and the Night of the Offering is once again upon us. You know what it means to be here. What's at stake. Remember, it is an honor to be chosen as an offering to ensure the safety of your people, and your name will be remembered for all time on the Stone of Shetan."

Chief Shaasi lifted her gaze to the top of Mount Traie, the tallest mountain on our island, where a huge slab of stone stood watching over us, its body etched with the names of those we'd already lost. She made it sound like an honor to have our names carved there, but really, the thing was a giant tombstone that loomed over us all—a constant reminder we could never escape our fates.

I thought of where I'd added Cara's name at the top of the stone. I'd been ten when I'd carved it, and the letters were more like an angry scrawl. Sadness mixed with anger bloomed inside me, but I knew the anger was mostly at myself. It was my fault my sister had been taken. *You'll find her even if it's the last thing you do.*

"Remember to stand tall, but don't look them in the eye, or they might see it as a challenge," the old crone continued. "If the Katakin wanted, they could wipe us from this island. We can't jeopardize the agreement between us, or we will all be lost. Your families and friends, brothers and sisters."

She paused, and her face became grave. "If you try to flee, you will have forsaken your people. You and your family will be banished from the island, doomed to die a watery death. And that's if the Katakin don't catch you first."

I rolled my neck as a chill night wind swept through the forest, fluttering the leaves of the nearby trees. A part of me appreciated how direct she was. What was the point of pretending this was going to turn out all right? If you were picked, you were fucked.

Either you were taken as an offering for the monsters and tortured for the remainder of your days, however long that was, or you were disgraced by the village and condemned with your family—all banished from the island. Which was also a death sentence.

The art of boat making had been lost to us years ago, and we only had a handful of rowboats remaining, which we used to go fishing in the shallows around our island. Those who went further out to sea never returned.

No one knew whether there was anything else out there, but with the frequent lightning storms crackling over the water every few nights, we all assumed the villagers who left the island died. If safe passage to a new land had been possible, we'd all have moved away by now.

That was not to say I hated it on the island. It was actually really beautiful. The air was always sweet with the smell of coconuts and summer fruits, waterfalls ran down from the mountains, and the ground and sea were fertile, so we never had to worry about starving. It was just unfortunate we were all stuck in this endless cycle of offerings to the Katakin monsters.

Chief Shaasi walked along our line, her back hunched and a twisted walking stick in her right hand. There were forty of us for the monsters to choose from this time. Forty young souls between the ages of eighteen and twenty-eight.

There were more of us between those ages, but they were exempt—either they were men (the monsters only requested females), or they were sisters of someone already in the lineup. For every eligible household with women aged between eighteen and twenty-eight, at least one woman had to participate in the Night of the Offering. If a household had more than one woman who was of selection age, only one had to participate.

Two hundred years ago, when the monster king and his warriors had first arrived, the king had been clear with his demand. Provide him with twelve beautiful women between the ages of eighteen and twenty-eight every ten years. If we couldn't deliver, he and his monsters would destroy us all. No one knew why the monster king had made an agreement with our ancestors at all, but I suspected they had to have some purpose for us. Some reason they needed fresh humans every ten years.

I peered at the long line of women standing next to me, ready to be sacrificed like animals waiting for slaughter. Tonight, twelve of us would be taken to become the playthings of monsters.

Or at least, that was what the elders said. No one who went with the monsters into the mouth of Procus, the massive cave that stared eerily at me from the other side of the clearing, ever came back.

For all we knew, those chosen were killed instantly. It was anyone's guess. Some of the villagers would say that sometimes for the weeks after the offering, they could hear screams when they went near the cave mouth, hence the rumor about them being tortured. I didn't know if this was true. I'd slept by the cave mouth for days after Cara had been taken, and I'd never heard a thing.

All we knew for sure was that twelve of us were offered up all so the rest of the villagers on the island could live...for another ten years. Until another offering. If one could call that living. *Goddess*, the idea made me want to stab something.

Chief Shaasi passed the first few in our line, pausing every now and then to chastise someone's clothing or tell them to fix their hair, even though everyone looked immaculate in garments far nicer than anything they'd ever owned. Apparently, soon after the offerings started all those years ago, some women had turned up to the Night of the Offering looking disheveled in the hopes it would decrease their chances of being chosen. The monsters had been insulted and enraged, and as punishment, they'd selected the twelve women they'd deemed acceptable and slaughtered the rest.

Now the whole village came together to make the garments for the Night of the Offering, and even I had to admit my own dress was spectacular. Like the material of the other women's garments, it was white, as supple as silk, and without a speck of dirt to be seen. White. The color of surrender and submission.

Bile rose in my throat, and I took a steadying breath, all too aware of the sweat beading on my brow. I couldn't lose my nerve now. I was the only insane person in this lineup who actually *wanted* to be chosen. No, correction, I *had* to be chosen. Only the most beautiful were selected, so there was the risk that I wouldn't be one of the twelve, but I was pretty enough, I hoped.

Thick red hair waved down my back, complementing my amber eyes and tanned skin, and I had the same hourglass shape as my sister. My looks were enough to draw attention from some of the men and women of the village, so I was hoping that was a good sign. Even if they called me a freak when they were with their friends.

Unlike them, I refused to accept my fate. Refused to accept my sister, *Cara's,* fate, and I think that scared them. I wasn't going to waste my time with useless skills like basket weaving and sewing like the other girls. I'd dedicated most of the last ten years to learning how to fight, training, and pushing my body to its limits. Cara was still alive, I could feel it, and I was going to save her. After she had been taken, I'd only had my father left, and he'd never said anything about me wanting to fight. I'm not sure if he really cared.

But the monsters were picky when they selected us. I didn't have some of the features they had seemed to favor in the women who'd been chosen in the past—hair as straight as a dagger and the color of midnight. No, I had... *The ability to stab a person in the eye from twelve feet away? Great. You'll definitely be chosen.*

I knew if anyone was sure to be selected, it would be Lana, with her straight black hair, porcelain skin, and breasts the size of coconuts. Lana towered over the two girls on either side of her further up the line, her white dress pulled so tightly against her that it looked three sizes too small. Everyone wanted Lana, and I couldn't blame them.

It was twisted, getting chosen. It was a major compliment to be selected—it showed you were the most beautiful and coveted—but at the same time, no one wanted to die.

Lana ran her fingers through her hair for what seemed like the thousandth time, then smoothed her hands down the front of her dress. It would be a huge blow to her ego if she wasn't chosen. Maybe she was as insane as I was and wanted to be selected as well?

Chief Shaasi stopped in front of me then, and I straightened as the old woman examined my appearance. We'd never had a great relationship, and I'm sure a part of her hoped I'd get chosen just so I'd stop being the pain constantly plaguing her. The oddity in her neatly organized village of sacrificial lambs. Well, for once, we both wanted the same thing.

I grinned at her innocently as she looked up and down my body. Her gaze lingered on my unruly hair, and she sniffed in disapproval before moving on to Yasmin, who stood next to me.

Turning away, I stared at the cave mouth before me. *The mouth of Procus.* I tried to swallow, but my throat was too dry. Possibly from all the training and running, or more likely because I felt as if I was peering into the giant eye of death.

The entrance was huge, at least the height of three average villagers and just as wide. Frowning, I stared into the darkness of the cave mouth, confused by the sudden appearance of six more lights.

Chief Shaasi shouted something from her position back in front of the line, but I didn't make out her words. I stood frozen because those weren't lights but *eyes* staring back at me—three pairs, to be exact. The glowing orbs moved toward me, becoming larger with every moment, and the hairs on the back of my neck stood on end.

The Katakin monsters had arrived.

CHAPTER 2

~ Raine ~

Violet, gold, and blue eyes advanced toward us steadily, the glowing lights dancing in the dark. My hands gripped the sides of my dress, and I wished I were holding one of my knives instead. Shifting my leg slightly, I was comforted by the weight of the small dagger I'd strapped high up on my thigh. But I didn't grab it out. I couldn't risk them seeing it. Not yet.

Where's the fourth monster? Everyone knew four monsters always appeared for the Night of the Offering. I strained my eyes, trying to make out the dark shapes, and as four forms emerged from the cave mouth, I realized why I hadn't noticed the last monster. Unnatural onyx-colored eyes with no white surrounding the pupils stared back at me, cold and predatory. Everything about that gaze screamed he was a hunter, a destroyer, and I clenched my jaw as I resisted the sudden instinct to run.

Power radiated from the four monsters and thickened the air as they advanced toward us, striding into the moonlight side by side. My knees shook, but I forced myself to assess the monsters with a sweeping gaze. *Pull it together, Raine.*

In the elders' tales, the monsters were grotesque, with horns thicker than a mountain goat's, pig snouts for noses, and bodies the height of giants. I blinked. While these four were all abnormally tall, they did not at all look like the monsters I'd always pictured in my mind. There were *definitely* no pig snouts.

Lifting my chin, I glared at the monster with the black eyes. His dark gaze was roving along the lineup, his full lips twisted into a cruel smile. Moonlight gleamed off his short raven-colored hair, the color contrasting against his pale, white skin. Huge black wings were folded behind his back, the skin leathery like giant bat wings, and a long sword was strapped to his side.

Arrogance oozed from the male, and his hands swung as he walked, his razor-sharp claws almost catching on the sides of the black leather coat covering his lean, muscular body. My stomach dropped as I imagined those claws easily shredding through flesh. *My* flesh. *I think I'm going to call you Asshole One.*

My gaze then went to the monster striding beside him, the one with glowing violet eyes. Small curved violet horns protruded from his shaggy coffee-colored hair, and a forked violet tail flicked behind him.

Easily the largest of the four, this monster was built like a boulder. Every inch of him was covered in sculpted muscle that bulged against his dark shirt and leather pants. *I'll definitely break my wrist if I punch that one. Right, blades only.* Axes rested on the sides of his hips, and I resisted the urge to roll my eyes. It was obvious he wouldn't need them with us puny humans. *Hello, Asshole Two.*

The third monster kept the gray hood of his cloak pulled low over his face, so I couldn't make out much besides his glowing blue eyes and the five silver stars pinned to the leather belt that crossed his chest.

His build was similar to the first monster's—lean and powerful. A lock of silver hair waved down the side of his neck like a glittering snake trailing along his collarbone. I had no doubt the monster was hiding some terrible secret beneath that hood, and I wasn't looking forward to finding out what it was. *I'll name you Asshole Three.*

The monsters came to a stop before our line, and the huge muscles of the fourth monster, *Asshole Four*, flexed as he folded his arms over his broad chest. He wasn't quite as bulky as Asshole Two but easily more muscular than One and Three.

His dark brows were pulled low, and furry pointed ears protruded from russet-colored hair. Narrowed golden eyes fixed their gaze on Chief Shaasi with a hatred that seemed to roll off him in waves, but despite the stern expression, he was easily as attractive as the other males, with a square jaw, tan skin, and an appealing slight cleft in his chin.

I looked at all four monsters again. Despite their unnatural height and some of their physical attributes, they looked almost human. Well, you know, if humans looked like they could shred you into ribbons or rip out a tree with one hand. The monsters were...*beautiful*. It was as if their bodies had been sculpted by the Goddess, Falia, herself and they had just walked down the steps from her haven.

Keep your head straight, I internally chastised myself. *These monsters are coming to lead you to your death. They're not taking you to their beds.* A low snort escaped me as I thought of the monsters taking the chosen villagers to their beds instead of to torture and death. Heck, no one had ever returned after leaving with the monsters, so for all I knew, the chosen might have been about to walk into a full-on orgy.

I nearly laughed outright then at my own outrageous thought as I imagined a disgusting amount of slippery bodies romping with these godlike monsters, but I managed to beat the sound back down, with only a strangled cough escaping me.

I thought the noise was quiet enough that no one would have heard, but I was wrong. Burning copper eyes fixed on me, holding my gaze, and the male monster's nostrils flared as if he was scenting the air. *Fuck.* I quickly lowered my head and stared at the ground. When Asshole Four didn't start lumbering toward me, I let out a slow breath. *Seriously? You want them to choose you, not slaughter you where you stand.*

"You know why we've come," a deep but smooth voice cracked through the air, coming from Asshole One, or A-One for short, the onyx-eyed monster. The other women in the lineup with me curled their shoulders to make themselves appear smaller. Gina, a pretty brunette standing two girls up from me, was so pale I was sure she would vomit at any moment. I pitied her, but there was nothing I could do. She just had to hope she wouldn't be chosen.

"Where's your leader?" A-One demanded, but by the way A-Four was back to glaring at Chief Shaasi, I was guessing they already knew. I'd heard the monsters lived much longer lives than humans. Was it possible these were the same monsters who had come for the collection years before? Had Chief Shaasi met them ten years ago? Had they taken Cara? I clenched my hands into fists at my sides.

Every gaze from my lineup turned toward Chief Shaasi, and the old woman stepped forward with a calm expression on her face. Despite her cool exterior, her thin frame seemed frail in comparison to the towering, muscular monsters glaring down at her.

"I am," Chief Shaasi said, and I admired the fact her voice didn't quaver.

"Are these the best you have to offer?" A-One's voice was harsh.

A-Three, the hooded monster with blue eyes, let out a low chuckle.

"Th-These are the most beautiful young women of our village," said Chief Shaasi, a slight stutter in her voice as she blinked in surprise. Her gaze went to Lana and then back to the onyx-eyed monster.

A-One's lip curled in disgust. "We came all the way here for this?"

Further up, Lana let out a small gasp and hung her head, a stray black strand falling over her face. Her hands were clasped together, and she fidgeted nervously.

My pity for her changed to anger as I turned my attention back to A-One. *Who the hell do these monsters think they are? If Lana's not good enough for them, there's no chance I'll be chosen.* I shifted my leg again, reminding myself of the dagger I'd hidden. If the monsters didn't honor the agreement and decided to slaughter the lot of us, I was at least going to try to take one of the fuckers down with me.

My gaze flicked over the four monsters in turn as I wondered whether I'd have a chance against any of them with my measly blade. If by some miracle the villagers and I managed to overpower these monsters, I could even still go into the mouth of Procus and try to find Cara. Would the cave still take me to their home if the monsters weren't with me? *Should I sever one of their heads to bring along just in case?* I grimaced. *Gross, Raine. Just gross.*

As my thoughts ran away with me, I didn't notice the onyx-eyed monster start strolling along our lineup until he stopped in front of a girl named Bri, with chestnut-colored hair that reached past her waist and a petite body. His voice was cold when he said, "You. Stand over there."

Oh, fuck.

Bri's legs wobbled as she obeyed and went to stand near the other monsters. She was cringing as if being near them was physically hurting her. I stared at her face, which was growing paler with each passing moment. Someone had been chosen. Bri was going to die. My nails bit into my palms, and my heart pounded.

A-One continued walking along our line, his long black coat almost dragging along the ground and his clawed hands folded behind him. He sneered as he scrutinized the next few people in the line until he stopped in front of Nora, a beautiful girl around twenty years old with almond-shaped brown eyes and shoulder-length black hair. "Step forward. You are chosen," A-One commanded.

Horror cut through me. Nora had five younger sisters, each of whom would miss her dearly. We'd been best friends once. Years ago, before Cara had been taken. I'd enjoyed having dinners with her and her sisters. The way she'd always made time to play with her youngest sibling was adorable. Losing her would destroy them. But Nora didn't hesitate. Stepping forward, she kept her chin up despite the fear that radiated from her. I knew it was fear for her family rather than for herself.

I hated this. I *hated* the monsters.

A-One continued to stride down the line, sometimes turning his head to stare back at the other monsters as if asking their opinion, to which they would answer with nods or shakes of their heads. By the time he neared my end of the line, ten villagers had already been chosen. Gina was the eleventh. That she hadn't vomited on the onyx-eyed monster when he'd stopped before her was a credit to her.

I watched as Gina went to stand near Lana and the other chosen. Lana had been selected earlier, and her legs shook as she stood there. For a moment, I thought Lana might collapse, but she remained standing. Clearly, she'd come to her senses and realized being tortured to death was not worth proving she was indeed one of the most beautiful in the village—even if she was ugly by monster standards.

I'd meant to keep my thoughts contained, but a giggle of hysterical laughter slipped from me. The idea that our village's most beautiful woman was uglier than a monster was just so ridiculous I couldn't help myself. I thought about all the effort we'd gone to in order to make ourselves presentable, only to be told we were insufficient. Though I guessed if all monsters looked like these four, perhaps we were uglier in comparison to their race. Realizing my mistake, I slapped my hand over my mouth. *Fuck. Too late.* Four sets of glowing eyes fixated on me.

A-One sidestepped from where he'd been looking down at a cowering Tanee, and he stopped in front of me. He leaned down, and the scents of cedarwood, ash, and spice filled my senses.

"Is there something you wish to say, human?" he articulated, emphasizing the word *human*. His top lip curled up to reveal a set of pointed white fangs.

"No," I managed weakly, my heart thudding so hard it was like a drumbeat in my ears.

"Oh, don't be shy now," the monster coaxed, his unnerving onyx-colored eyes never leaving my face.

Sweat pooled between my breasts, and I shifted under his gaze. This was my only chance to be chosen. My one chance to find Cara. *Fuck, please don't eat me. Or maybe that wouldn't be so bad? Wait, what?* Heat flooded my cheeks as my brain scrambled to hold on to a coherent thought with the absurdly sexy but undeniably dangerous monster looming over me. I was clearly losing my mind.

"I just—" I began. A small voice inside me screamed at me to run. To hike up my dress and hightail it the fuck out of there, but I couldn't. The Katakin would just catch me, and if they didn't, my father and I would be banished from the island and would die out at sea anyway. *You want to be chosen, remember?*

I tried to calm my racing pulse and racked my brain for something to say that wouldn't anger the monster enough that he would cut me down. Something that might make me more alluring. *What do monsters want to hear? Flattery? Insults?* I swallowed as the monster's stare became impatient. *Fuck it, the truth it is.* "Erm, it's funny," I blurted.

In the span of a heartbeat, A-One's hand shot out, his long fingers curling around my neck and squeezing. The clack of claws sounded, but they didn't pierce my flesh. "Funny?" The monster's voice was lethal, and he raised a questioning dark brow.

Pain traveled down my neck, and any bravery I'd had dissolved instantly. I realized it then. I was going to die. The understanding was swift, but hell, if I was going out, I figured I might as well dish out some hard truths while I was at it.

I bared my teeth in a half-smile, half-choked grimace. "Yeah, fun-ny. It's funny you're sneering at us for being ugly, and yet you're the fucking monsters."

A few of the others in the lineup gasped loudly.

I waited for the blow. Perhaps the swift snap of my neck or an obliterating pain in my chest as the monster ripped my heart out. I could taste the fear on my tongue.

The monster tipped his head back, his fangs protruding from his lips. *Maybe he'll drink my blood until I'm drained like a husk?* I'd never heard of a monster doing that, but surely those pointed teeth weren't just for eating potatoes.

Closing my eyes, I prepared myself for the worst, but the sudden sound of laughter made me flinch. Opening my eyes, I gaped. A-One was laughing, his head tipped back and the sound rich and haughty with the ring of true amusement. When his laughter finally died down, he turned to the other monsters. "This human thinks *we're* the ugly ones," he said incredulously.

My muscles tensed as I watched the others, but I was surprised to find A-Two had a shit-eating grin, A-Three simply cocked his head to the side, and A-Four, well his glare remained hard, but he didn't look like he was bothered by the comment.

Before I realized what was happening, A-One leaned forward again, his lips and the tips of his fangs close to my ear. "Step forward, *beautiful*. I'm going to enjoy devouring you," he whispered, mocking me with the nickname.

My mouth dried out, and a shiver clawed its way down my spine. I was okay with death. I had no one relying on me anyway. And I didn't for a second believe the monster actually thought I was beautiful, but...devouring? Did he mean he was actually going to eat me or...? My cheeks flushed further, and my core heated.

I hated that the monster had me feeling all sorts of confusing things. Did he have a power that was messing with my emotions, my mind? *And who the hell tells a monster they're ugly?* I internally scolded myself.

"We're done here," A-One called out to the other monsters and began striding away from the lineup. I followed him, fighting against the sickening feeling in the pit of my stomach. I'd gotten what I wanted, but now I wasn't so sure if that was a good thing.

The other chosen villagers stepped into place behind us, and the other monster assholes took up the rear, shepherding us toward Procus. I only managed to glimpse the pained look on Chief Shaasi's wrinkled face before we stepped into the darkness of the cave mouth.

Our group walked forward in the pitch black for what felt like ages, with only the sounds of our panicked breathing and the shuffling of our feet breaking the silence. How we managed not to fall into each other, I suspected, was the monsters doing. The fuckers could probably see in the dark.

When we rounded a corner, I halted, knowing why we'd stopped. In the years after Cara had been taken, I'd brought a torch with me and explored every inch of this cave. This was as far as I'd ever come because here a huge boulder blocked the cave, tightly fitting to the walls so there was no way through.

I heard a grunt and the scrape of stone, and then blue light spilled into the tunnel, illuminating the darkness. A-Two's frame came into view as he pushed the boulder forward, making a gap for us to walk through, the blue light outlining his body. *I knew it!* I'd always believed there had to be a way through, but I'd never figured out how to get the boulder to budge, and none of the other villagers had been willing to help me. They thought it would anger the monsters if we disrupted the silence of the cave.

I stared, unable to believe my eyes as I stepped past the boulder to see a huge ring of blue fire that burned before us. The circle was almost the size of the cave, blue flames licking at the walls. Lana bumped into me from behind, and gasps and whispers erupted from the other women.

Has this always been here? I didn't have time to contemplate the question. A-One's fingers wrapped firmly around my arm, and he yanked me forward into the portal, his claws barely missing my flesh.

Blinding pain shot through me as I tumbled into darkness, the hard press of fingers on my arm the only sensation reminding me I wasn't dead...yet.

CHAPTER 3

~ Raine ~

I was falling. Or at least, that was what it felt like. As if I was being thrown between the hands of giants with nothing to cling to.

As quickly as it came, the pain subsided, and I was left spinning. Blue light swirled around me, the vibrant color almost too much for my eyes to bear, and I squeezed my eyes shut as I fought against my roiling stomach.

My ears popped at the exact moment my feet planted on something hard, the air turning chilly and the world seeming to still. I breathed in, taking in the dank air and scent of dampened soil and blinked, somehow knowing we were now someplace else.

I didn't have the chance to take in my surroundings. The hand that was clamped around my arm pulled me forward, and I twisted my head to the left in time to see a flash of A-One's onyx-colored eyes and a cruel smile before he pushed me forward and released me.

And then I was falling again. This time, an uncomfortable sensation made it feel as though my stomach left me as I careened down what seemed to be a huge pit, plummeting toward the darkness below.

Terror ripped a scream from my throat, but the sound was gobbled up by the air. I looked up as flashes of white appeared high above me as the other villagers were also thrown over the edge of whatever ledge we'd been on.

The shouts and screams of the other villagers grounded my thoughts, and I pushed through my fear, my survival instincts kicking in. Reaching out wildly, I tried to grab at the crumbling stone wall to my right, but only air passed through my fingers. My thoughts became frantic as I tried to think of another option.

Was this our torture? Maybe we'd keep falling for eternity? It was possible, but something in A-One's glare made me think this couldn't be it. I'd insulted them all, I'd called them ugly, and I was sure they had something else planned for me.

While that thought should have terrified me, in this moment, it gave me hope. If this wasn't our end, it meant there had to be a way out. Either that, or I was completely wrong, and maybe I'd eventually hit the bottom like an egg on a pan. *Definitely not going to be able to eat eggs for a while.*

That was my last thought as my feet broke through frigid water, and the stifling cold swallowed me whole.

Water gushed into my mouth before I had the sense to seal my lips shut, and within moments, my lungs were burning. There were no shadows in the water. Nothing to tell me where to swim to, so I simply tried swimming in the direction I hoped was up. I pumped my arms furiously, using every ounce of strength I had. With each swipe, I hoped my fingers would break the surface, but only water surrounded my numb body.

My arms reached out again, every muscle aching, but still...nothing. I was unable to control my own body, and my mouth burst open, more water rushing in. My body bucked as it tried to expel the liquid. *Well, fuck. This happened quicker than I thought.*

My eyes slowly closed, and I waited for the embrace of death. Just as darkness hollowed out my mind, strong fingers pressed against my flesh and hauled me out of the water before dropping me heavily onto icy stone.

My eyelids sprang open, and I rolled to my side as huge, racking coughs exploded from me, and water poured from my throat. My shoulders heaved as I retched, and I could feel eyes on me, but I didn't care. I was *alive.*

When I could breathe normally again, I stared around at the other villagers and counted them as they were tossed from the water onto the rock shelf with me. *Nine. No, wait. Ten.* My gaze swept frantically around at the villagers.

Gina was there, and so was Bri and Nora. But... *Lana.* My blood went cold.

Peering back at the water, I squinted, hoping desperately that she would appear, but the black water was now eerily still, the surface as smooth as glass. *No.* Lana and I weren't friends. Far from it, but she didn't deserve this.

She was gone. Likely *dead.* A cold numbness wrapped around me. Whether we were just deep underground or in a different world altogether, I had no clue. I only knew one thing with certainty. *No one will ever know what happened to her.*

Sadness swirled within me, and I looked away from the other villagers and to the top of the pit, where the faintest tinge of blue could be seen. Whatever it was that had brought us here, that strange magical doorway, it was up there. When I found Cara, we'd have to find a way to get to it.

I forced my back to straighten and turned to glare at the monsters, who watched us from nearby. A-Two stood with his hands resting on the ends of his ax handles, and A-Four had his arms crossed in front of his chest. *Where are the other two?*

As if he'd heard my thought, A-One appeared from a stone archway further to the left. His black gaze connected with mine, and he smirked. I wished I could slap the smug smile off his face. *Cara. Remember, you're here for Cara.* I said the words internally like a mantra. I could do this.

But as A-One stepped closer to me, my pulse began racing again. It was as if there was a force inside me telling me to go to him. Telling me that I *needed* him. *What the hell?* I didn't need him, but my body was telling me otherwise. *Fuck.* I'd never really thought of the fact that the monsters might have magic. It was the only explanation for how I was feeling, and it was going to make my whole rescue mission a lot harder.

A-One stopped alongside the other monsters, but his gaze remained fixed on me. *Seriously, this is your own fault, Raine. If you hadn't called them ugly, they might not have paid much attention to you.*

"Please, I'll do anything. Please, please don't kill me," a trembling voice cried out, and I turned to see Gina sobbing as she crawled toward the monsters on her hands and knees. Her wet dress was plastered to her skin, making her look fragile and almost naked.

I ground my jaw as A-One's gaze flicked to her, and his expression darkened as he stared down at the shivering girl.

Get up, Gina, I pleaded. *Get up before he kills you.*

I stared at the two villagers closest to her, hoping one of them would reach out and pull her to her feet. They looked at her but made no move to help, their own fear freezing them in place.

"Rise, human," A-Four growled, his rumbling voice echoing around the space.

"I–I can do things. I can clean or cook. Anything!" Gina's voice became shrill.

"To your feet," A-Four said, but Gina just sobbed harder, her shoulders shaking.

I swallowed as dread unfurled inside me. I had to do something. *You've already drawn too much attention. Remember why you're here.* I chewed on the inside of my cheek, biting hard enough to taste the bitter tang of blood.

My gaze found Nora's, and my dread was mirrored in her eyes, but she shook her head at me—a small, almost imperceptible shake. *You can't help her.* I could hear her silent words.

"I hate it when they grovel," A-One said with disgust. He stepped forward, a clawed hand outstretched toward a wide-eyed, sniffling Gina.

Fuck it. There was a reason I was called a freak back on the island. I was never happy to just follow the rules.

"Keep your damn hands to yourself," I said as I shot forward, moving in front of Gina. I'd meant to sound confident, but my words were a quiet rasp, my throat still raw from throwing up half the lake. If that was even what the hell the black water was.

Shock flared on A-One's face, and his hand hovered in the air. Assholes Two and Four remained seemingly relaxed, but I noticed the hardening of their bodies as if they were about to spring into action. *Shit.*

"You good there, Locke?" Amusement lit the horned monster's eyes.

Locke. I took note of the name.

A-One's, *Locke's*, expression hardened as he stared at me, a sparkle of something dangerous in his black eyes. When he spoke again, his gaze remained on me, but his voice rang around the dank space. "You all belong to us now. If we want to hurt you, we can. If we want to starve you, we can. And if we want to...touch you..." His gaze lowered to my chest, and I looked down to see what he was staring at. My hard nipples poked out from my soaked dress, puckered from the cold. *Fucking. White. Dress.* I glared back at him, refusing to be embarrassed. The monster smirked. "We can," he finished, his voice lowering.

My nostrils flared as heat once again bloomed in my cheeks, a strange thrill going through me as my gaze dipped to Locke's ridiculously perfect lips. *What is wrong with me?* I should have been scared. And I should have learned my lesson about insulting and defying monsters.

At least the monster's attention was away from Gina. I tried to think only of the dagger still strapped tightly to my inner thigh, but then I was thinking about the monster's lips kissing my thigh instead. *How much would it hurt if he bit me?*

Shit. I seriously needed help.

In a flash of movement, cold fingers wrapped around my arm, and once again, I was being yanked forward by the monster.

"The rest of you... Move!" A-Four barked right in my ear as we passed him. *Asshole. Sexy, fucking assholes.*

Locke led me into a dark tunnel, and the torches on the rocky walls flared to life with blue fire as we neared, illuminating the darkness. I let the monster pull me along, ignoring the painful grip of his hand on my arm. The shuffle of feet behind me told me the others from my village were following closely behind.

Eventually, we started passing huge iron doors. Locke finally stopped at one on the right and wrenched the door open. Releasing my arm, he pushed me inside the darkened room. Torches around the space instantly ignited, showing bare rocky walls, a cot to one side, a small wooden table, and another door at the back.

I swung around. "What is this?" I hissed.

"You failed the first test," he said, his voice smooth and mocking.

My brow creased. "Failed?"

He grinned widely, baring his fangs. "Welcome to the monster trials, *beautiful*."

And he slammed the door in my face.

CHAPTER 4

~ Locke ~

"I swear, I don't know who's being tested more—the humans or us—because it's a test of my willpower to not just kill them all," I snarled as I slammed the door, carelessly letting my clawed hands scratch the iron. I rolled my neck as my claws retracted into my fingertips, my wings disappeared, and the whites returned to my eyes. *I'd be doing them a fucking mercy.*

More of the villagers had begged and pleaded as they'd been led to their rooms, and I couldn't stand the pathetic whine of their voices. It wouldn't be for long, I knew. They'd change soon. And with that would come a whole new challenge. But at least they wouldn't be my problem then.

"How can beings be so fucking weak?" I grumbled, pulling off my sword. I hung it near the door, finding a space on the long rack already overflowing with weapons.

Asher watched with an amused grin from where he stood leaning against the mantel, blue firelight illuminating his short, violet horns and a goblet in his hand. Darian raised a silver brow at me where he lounged next to a stern-faced Kade on a plush red settee. Kade was back in his human form, his ears rounded again and his fangs nowhere to be seen. The only one who couldn't hide his monstrous side was Asher.

Kade's eye twitched, and my frown deepened. I knew that look. A lecture was coming. *Fuck me.*

"What?" I snapped, stalking into the room and sinking onto the unoccupied settee closest to the fire.

Before Kade had a chance to respond, Darian said, "Are you sure it's all of the humans you want to kill or, perhaps, a specific one? Say, a very *beautiful* one with a feisty attitude, who happens to think we're all ugly?" Darian's cloak had been discarded, and his long silver hair reflected the glow of the fire.

My eyes narrowed, and I became thoughtful at the mention of the woman with the fiery temper. After her outburst in the clearing, I couldn't help but pick her. She was a breath of fresh air in an otherwise stifling situation. But when we'd crossed through the portal and I'd pushed her into the pit, I couldn't deny that I felt something...strange.

Her rapid heartbeat filled my ears, like a siren call telling me to swoop down and snatch her up. I could feel the fear of all the villagers, but hers was different. It was as if the human was calling to me, and my entire body wanted to respond. An uncomfortable pain had sprouted in my chest, and it had taken all my effort to stay where I'd been watching them.

When Darian had rescued the villagers from the water, the pain had soon subsided, and I wondered if I'd imagined it. Still, the whole situation had me on edge. Despite this, my lips quirked into a smile. "That girl has a death wish."

Asher chuckled. "Hope you know what you're doin' picking that one."

Darian plucked at the cheese on the table in front of him and leaned back, crossing one leg over the other. "If he didn't, I would have," he drawled. "I thought these trials would be a bore. It's nice to see a human with an actual backbone. Perhaps they're not all weak after all."

Kade leaned forward, resting his elbows on his knees and gripping his goblet.

Here it comes. I braced myself for his tirade. Kade was often the voice of reason in our group.

"We're not here to have fun," Kade growled. "No matter how attractive you might find the human. There'll be time for that during the Week of Orash if you're that keen. For now, we have to get this done."

He didn't have to remind me. I was the one who informed my brothers we'd been assigned to carry out the job of selecting the humans.

Darian rolled his eyes at Kade. "Yes, yes, we're here to show we're capable of doing something other than drinking and fucking for a change," he said with a dismissive wave of his hand.

"And killin'," Asher added with an eager grin.

Kade's jaw clenched. "Speak for yourself, Darian. I know how to keep my cock in my pants."

"One down," I said coldly, my mind still thinking of the humans. "Eleven to go."

"One always changes during the first test, Locke," Asher commented. "Don't know why you expected any different."

I remained silent for a moment, my brow furrowed. "It's been ten years. I had hoped…"

"That's your problem, brother," Kade growled. "Hoping. In two hundred years, the curse hasn't changed. Anyone who comes here turns within days. This will be the same as the last time and the time before that."

"This mountain will always turn humans into monsters," Darian said with a somber look.

"Remind me, who lasted the longest the last time?" Asher asked.

Kade let out a long breath and took a swig from his goblet before answering. "A human who became a wolf. She lasted four nights before she changed. A new record. Her name's Olive."

Four fucking nights. We remained quiet, with only the crackle of the fire breaking the silence. I wondered what abomination the fiery woman with the ludicrously tempting body would turn into. Her amber eyes burned in my mind, and the scent of her still haunted my senses, almost making me drool. *Have my brothers noticed how fucking good she smells?*

My fangs started to elongate at the thought, and I kept my lips clamped shut. It had been a long time since anyone had almost broken my control. This human didn't know just how fine a line she was walking. And in that almost see-through dress...

Asher downed the remainder of his goblet and pushed off from the wall. "Better get some sleep. I'm up tomorrow. The humans have no idea what's coming." Grabbing a bread roll from the table, he left for one of the adjoining rooms, closing his door behind him.

"Where's the lovely new vampire?" Darian asked, bringing my attention back.

Irritated, I remembered watching the villagers as they'd fallen down the pit of Reask, their bodies white blurs against the black. I'd been busy staring at the amber-eyed human when another villager had disappeared from my peripheral vision. It was the dark-haired one with an attractive but slightly sour face. Black wings had torn through her white dress, and she'd flown to the top of the pit, instinctively drawn to me. I scowled.

"I sent her on," I replied as I pulled a small vial from my coat and downed the synthetic blood, ignoring the bitter aftertaste. It did nothing to dampen my craving for fresh blood.

The villager had become one of the worst, unfortunately for her. Having an eternal thirst that nothing could quench made life a living hell. My brothers didn't know how lucky there were to have turned into other monsters, though I supposed they had their own torments.

The four of us used the term "brother" frequently, but we weren't brothers by blood. We were just the closest things we had to a real family. Easily more so than the bloodsucking abominations who were my father and mother. "She's the Taratun council's problem now," I said, bringing my thoughts back to the villager. "Taming the first nights of bloodlust from a newly turned isn't my job."

Darian hummed in agreement. "And thank the devils for that."

Downing my second vial of blood, I pocketed the empty glass tubes. "I need a soak," I muttered, rising to my feet. *A fucking cold one.*

An image of the amber-eyed human standing defiantly in front of me with her see-through dress plastered to her breasts appeared in my mind. *Beautiful.* My lip twitched upward. She likely thought I was mocking her with the nickname, but she was fucking sexy. And whatever was drawing me toward her was dangerous. I had enough of my own problems. I didn't need any more. I needed to get the hell away from her.

I strode toward the washroom but paused when I remembered the pain I'd felt when I was going through portal. It had been brutal but fleeting.

Flexing my right hand, I stretched out my fingers. At first, I'd wondered if the human had zapped me with magic. It was possible she had already started to turn into a monster, and had used her newfound power on me. But when I touched her for the second time, the feeling hadn't returned. *What if the portal's damaged?* Cold dread filled me.

Frowning, I turned back around. "Kade."

My wolf brother lifted his head.

"When you have a moment, check out the portal. I felt something...strange when we were passing through."

Kade's brows pulled low. "I didn't feel anything unusual." He paused, and then anger sparked in his eyes. "You think the fae could have messed with it?"

Of course, his thoughts went straight to the fae. "I don't know," I said honestly. "It could be that the magic of the portal is starting to wane."

"If the portal closes, we are truly done for." Darian blew out a breath and popped a grape into his mouth.

Kade nodded. "I'll take a look."

CHAPTER 5

~ Raine ~

I glared at the closed door, then turned to face the room. I didn't want to think about all the horrible things A-One, or Locke, was planning to do to me. What the hell were the monster trials? Was this some sort of game to them? And where were the others from my village? If I stopped to think about it all, I was sure fear and exhaustion would have consumed me, but I had no time for that. I couldn't let Cara down.

So instead, I focused on the here and now and peered at my surroundings. Small torches of blue fire lined the walls, but they were up too high for me to reach. *Shame. I could use more weapons.*

My gaze swept over the simple cot with a blanket and a small table with a pitcher of pale-pink liquid. A cup sat upturned beside it. Striding over, I sniffed the liquid, and my brow creased when I detected a faint floral smell. I knew most of the forest flowers back on the island, but I couldn't place the scent. *Nice try, monster assholes. You can keep your poison, thank you.*

Ignoring the pitcher, I turned my attention to the narrow door at the back of the room. Pulling my dagger from my thigh, I held it up. I couldn't be sure what was behind there, and I wanted to be ready. Cautiously, I swung the door open, and light flooded the small space at the movement.

I peered into the washroom, and my shoulders relaxed when I saw no one else was in there. *Thank the goddess.* Lowering my blade, I slid it back into the sheath strapped to my thigh. *At least the monsters aren't treating us completely like animals.* There wasn't a bath, but there was at least somewhere I could relieve myself.

Going back into the main room, I started running my hands over the cool, rocky walls. I wasn't the first person to use the room. Scratches carved the stone, and faint splatters of blood appeared around the space. I tried not to think about what had caused the blood or who it had come from.

When I had finished my inspection of the walls, I turned my attention to the cot, first checking under the blanket and then kneeling to check underneath the frame. *Nothing.* I tried to contain my disappointment. Had I really been foolish enough to think I might find another weapon or a hidden tunnel?

The sound of steps outside my room had me jumping back to my feet. Before I'd had a chance to remove my dagger, black smoke curled under the crack of the door and reached toward me like clawed fingers. I slapped a hand over my mouth and nose, but the smoke wrapped around my face, and then I was pulled into darkness.

· · · ● · ● · ● · · ·

Crouching low behind the tree, I suppressed a giggle. The old crone, Chief Shaasi, had almost seen me poking my head out of the shadows, but when she spotted nothing unusual, she let out a huff and turned her attention away from my location. I'll be in so much trouble if she catches me, *I thought excitedly.*

I waited a moment, then dared to peek from behind the tree again. A long line of villagers stretched across the clearing, and I marveled at their pretty clothes, the silky white sparkling in the moonlight as if they were daughters of the Goddess, Falia. They'd been out there since sunset, and I still hadn't seen any monsters. I grinned, my smile so wide my cheeks hurt. The others were going to be so jealous when I told them I'd seen a monster.

"Rainie, you shouldn't be out here!" a girl's voice hissed behind me almost making me jump.

I turned to see Cara watching me, concern pulling at her hazel eyes. Her sleek mousey-brown hair was tousled from sleep, and goose bumps prickled on her skin, her white nightgown doing nothing to protect against the cold night air.

"I won't be long," I whispered. I'd thought I'd been quiet when I'd left her sleeping in our shared bed and crept out of the window. She must have woken after I was gone. "I just want to see if they're real. Did you know Elder Hinter said some of them have wings?"

Cara yanked on the back of my flimsy nightgown. "It's forbidden. We need to get back to the cottage. Father will—"

"They'll never see me," I pleaded, cutting her off. "Please, Cara, I just want a quick look." I gave her my puppy-dog eyes, though I doubted they would have their full effect in the shadows.

She sighed heavily. "It's too dangerous, Rainie," she said, sticking her hands under my armpits and pulling, forcing me to stand. "The Katakin will be here soon. We have to go."

"I just want to see—" I protested as I wriggled out of her grip. My weight wasn't balanced properly, and I tripped, snapping a branch from the tree as I fell to the ground in a crumpled heap.

A bloodcurdling howl pierced the air, and my heart jumped to my throat as I realized what I'd done. "Is this an ambush?" a deep voice bellowed from the clearing, and I heard the zing of steel.

Cara gasped, and I turned back to her. My eyes widened with horror as I saw her rooted to the spot, away from the cover of the tree and bathed in the moonlight. I must have pushed her back when I'd tripped. Her terrified gaze connected with mine.

"Who's this skulking in the trees, your little spy?"

I couldn't see who was speaking, but the rasp of his voice made my body quake with fear.

"No, no, of course not." Chief Shaasi spoke this time. "You know children. It can be hard to get them to follow the rules. Step out of the trees, girl."

Cara's body shook as she took a step toward the clearing. I was still sprawled on my stomach, only just obscured by the tree, and I tried to reach out and grab her other ankle.

"Stay hidden. They haven't seen you yet," she whispered, her voice so soft I could barely hear it.

Tears pricked at my eyes. "You're only sixteen. They can't take you."

She swallowed thickly. "Whatever happens, you keep your eyes shut and don't move, all right?"

"But—"

"Promise me."

My bottom lip trembled, but I nodded.

"Now, girl!" Chief Shaasi snapped, and Cara startled and stepped into the clearing.

I couldn't move. Fear gripped me, and I struggled to breathe. Struggled to think. I didn't hear what they were saying. I kept waiting, thinking Cara would eventually walk back to me, but she never came. By the time I was able to move again and looked out from behind the tree, a group of villagers were already shuffling toward the mouth of Procus, shepherded by massive, hooded figures.

Tears ran down my cheeks when I spotted Cara in her nightgown at the front of the group. And then she had stepped through into the cave mouth, a hooded figure pushing her forward with a gray hand on her back.

"Cara!" I screamed and scrambled to my feet. My desperation broke through my fear, and I sprinted across the clearing as fast as my ten-year-old legs would carry me. All the chosen villagers had entered the cave mouth now, and the last hooded figure turned back to look at me.

His glowing yellow eyes watched me from the darkness, and then he was gone.

CHAPTER 6

~ Raine ~

My eyes snapped open, and I sucked in a gasping breath as I bolted upright. Light flooded the room as the torches on the walls flared to life at my movement, and I closed my eyes with a wince. *One. Two. Three.* I counted the breaths as I sucked in air. *It was just a memory. Breathe, Raine. Just breathe.*

When my pounding heartbeat finally calmed, I remembered the black smoke that had seeped under the door.

What had—? My hands shot to my chest. *Still dressed.*

I was also still in what appeared to be the same room, except now I was positioned on the cot and my wet dress had made the blanket damp.

I twisted to look around me and grimaced when I moved my arm. An angry red dot was situated on the inner crease, and I prodded it with my finger, surprised by the small sting of pain at the touch. *What did they do to me?*

My heart rate spiked again when I thought about my dagger. If the monsters had come here while I slept, had they found it? My hand dropped to my thigh, and I blew out a breath of relief when I felt the handle through the fabric of my dress. *Too close.* I had to get out of there and find Cara.

Crusty bread had been left on a platter near the pink liquid, the only other sign that I'd had a visitor. Lifting the bread to my nose, I found it smelled much the same as what we had back home. No hint of anything strange, like the floral scent in the water. I couldn't be sure it wasn't poisoned, but I needed my strength. *Who knows when I'll see food again.* Hoping for the best, I nibbled it, surprised to find it tasted fresh and helped ease my queasy stomach.

When I finished the bread, I eyed the pink liquid, all too aware of my dry throat. But I didn't drink. They wouldn't get me that easily. Not yet, anyway.

With a little of my energy renewed, I took a breath, drew my dagger, and waited to the side of the door.

· · · ● · ● · · ·

A fist thumped on the iron door of my room, and my muscles tensed. I was ready to get out of this hell hole.

"Your turn, Sharachi," a deep masculine voice called from the other side.

Sharachi? I tightened my fingers on the hilt of my dagger.

The door swung open, and I didn't let myself hesitate. I shot forward, driving my dagger into the solid body entering the room. In a split second, strong hands lashed out, sending me flying across the space. I landed in a heap to the side of the cot, pain jarring up my limbs, and I bit my lip to stifle a groan. *Well, that didn't go as planned.*

Lifting my aching head, I focused my swirling vision to stare at where the horned monster stood inside the doorway, my dagger jutting from his muscled shoulder. My lip twitched up. *Not a total failure.* Though, it seemed wrong to mar such a stunningly chiseled body.

A-Two stared at the dagger, then pulled it out in one swift motion as if it were nothing but a splinter. Black blood coated the blade, but I didn't have time to contemplate the color. My eyes widened as I watched his wound close and the skin stitch back together. *This fucker is indestructible.* I'd always assumed that the monsters were different to humans, but I hadn't expected that. *All right, so my plans of escape just got a little harder.*

A-Two strode toward me, the muscles on his bare arms rippling in the light, and I shuffled back until I bumped against the side of the cot. *Fuck.* Instinctively, I lifted my arms to block his lethal blow. There was no way I'd survive a hit by a monster that size, and I knew it, but there was nothing around me to use as a weapon and nowhere for me to go.

I waited for the blow. Waited for the pain that had to be coming, but... nothing happened. Frowning, I moved my arms away from my face and blinked in surprise at A-Two's outstretched hand.

"Sorry 'bout that," he said shrugging sheepishly, and his lips molded into a wide grin. "Acted on instinct. Lucky I didn't use all my strength, or I would've killed ya."

"I—what?" Confusion dampened my anger. *Did he just...apologize?*

I went to ignore his outstretched hand, but he grabbed my arm and began pulling me to my feet. The moment his fingers touched me, pain crackled up my arm and traveled through my body, the sensation taking my breath away. With a wince, I yanked my arm away.

"What the hell did you do to me?" I accused when the pain left me, and I could breathe again.

He shook his head, his shaggy coffee-colored hair flicking around his violet eyes, and I could have sworn there was genuine shock on his face. Slowly, his frown morphed back into a smile. "Dar was right. You're goin' to be fun."

Goddess, these monsters are infuriating. Nothing that comes out of their mouths ever makes any sense. I don't know why I expected any different. With a huff, I eyed my dagger which looked ridiculously small grasped in A-Two's hand.

He held the blade in front of him, poised before his chest, and without thinking, my gaze wandered to the hard muscles across his broad shoulders. Just like with Locke, A-One, it was as if there was something pulling me toward him. Telling me to get close to him. To run my fingers along the sculpted muscle of his arms. To...

"I'd better hang on to this, though," A-Two added, pulling me from whatever strange state I'd been in.

I blinked rapidly, startled at where my mind had gone. At the ache that was inside me. My thoughts were clearer again, but there was still the feeling. Like I had to get closer to this monster.

Fuck that. I mean, sure I could appreciate the male was handsome as hell, even with the horns and tail, but no way was I that foolish. No, the asshole was messing with my mind just like Locke had. He had to be. I wouldn't let him rattle me.

Glaring, I didn't say anything as A-Two slid my dagger into the side of his leather pants, and I took a mental note of the name he'd just mentioned. *Dar.* He had to be talking about another one of the monsters who'd gone to my island.

"Well, now that you've had your fun, shall we?" He smiled and casually gestured toward the door.

When I continued to glare at him, he strode through the doorway, his large steps taking him swiftly down the tunnel. Of course, the arrogant monster knew I would follow him.

Hurrying from my room, I caught up to him and fell into step behind. He didn't bother turning to look at me when I joined him, but I had no doubt he knew I was there.

I eyed the handle of my dagger bobbing above his leather pants as he walked. My fingers twitched as I thought of how easily I could grab it, but I snuffed out the thought. If I grabbed it, he'd be on me in a moment, and then what?

Having momentarily given up on the idea, I let my gaze wander, and I found myself staring at his ridiculously perfect ass. The black leather pulled tight with each stride, molding to each cheek and giving me a sinful view.

As if he could feel my gaze, he turned his head to peer at me. Quickly, I forced my attention to his face, but his knowing smirk told me he knew I'd been perving. My cheeks flushed with heat, but I gave him my best "so what?" face.

Shaking his head, he let out a low chuckle. "*Lots* of fun," he muttered under his breath.

Holy goddess, what the hell is wrong with me?

The walk seemed never-ending until we veered off to the right down an even narrower tunnel and entered a wide cavern. Sand crunched under my feet as we crossed to the middle of the room. Again, the torches lining the walls were up much too high for me to reach, but in this cavern, a space for each torch had been carved out of the wall.

My brows knitted as I took in the empty room. "Where are the others?"

"Others?" A-Two responded, turning to look at me.

I resisted the urge to roll my eyes. He had to know who I was talking about. "The other villagers," I clarified.

"Oh, they've already been," he said casually.

What the hell does that mean? But then I saw the blood splatters and footprints scattered across the sand, and my stomach plummeted. I clenched my jaw, grinding my teeth together. "If you killed them...," I seethed.

He lifted a brow and didn't bother hiding his amused smile. "Then I don't doubt you'd try to avenge them."

"Well, did you?"

"They're still breathing," he said with a shrug. His gaze flicked across the cavern, and I turned to see he was staring at nothing but a bare part of the cavern wall. Frowning, I wondered whether he was trying to tell me something. *Are the villagers behind the wall?* The notion was absurd, but anything was possible in this place.

He turned his attention back to me, a mischievous glint in his eyes. "I've been looking forward to watchin' you dance. We all have. If anything's goin' to make you change, it'll be this. Have fun, Sharachi."

Watching me dance, what does—? Before I even had the chance to try and decipher his words, he was striding back toward the door. I only had enough time to yell, "My name's not Sharachi!" just before the iron door slammed shut. *Make me change?* I'd barely turned the question over in my mind when I found myself gaping as the door disappeared into the gray stone wall of the cavern as if it had never been there in the first place. All that was left was me, a human, on the bloodied sand.

My hands grew clammy as I scanned the cavern again. *Goddess, I wish the asshole hadn't taken my dagger. All right, so it probably wouldn't have helped me much, but it would have been something.* My internal whine died as a strange creaking noise sounded, and my gaze shot upward. High above, a hidden panel shifted in the ceiling, and then something was falling right toward me. I sidestepped just in time to avoid the small stone that would have smacked onto my skull.

The rock thudded to the ground, and I stared in disbelief as it was sucked into the sand and disappeared from sight. *Well, that's not good.* I squinted as if hoping to see some small detail I was missing, like you know, absolutely anything that made sense about this whole situation, but another creak from above drew my attention.

Another falling rock careened toward me, and I dodged to the side to avoid it. Like the other one, it was also eaten by the sand, and a sickening feeling wormed through my gut. This one was larger than the last—half the size of my clenched fist.

I looked at where the door had been only moments earlier, and I darted over, running my fingers along the bare rocky wall. When I found there were no hidden grooves indicating a door, just smooth, cold stone, I let out a growl of frustration. A creaking sounded overhead, and I jumped away from the wall as a third rock fell from the ceiling, thudding onto the sand inches from my toes.

A-Two's words came to me as I stared at the rock sinking into the sand like the others had. *If anything's goin' to make you change, it'll be this.* Again, I asked myself the question: *Change into what?*

Rolling my shoulders, I peered upward as another creak sounded from above, and I moved quickly to the side. I'd been running around the island since Cara had been taken, knowing that an agile body was often the key to survival. Whatever this sick game of the monsters was, I could dodge a few rocks.

If they all wanted to see me sweat, fine. But I'd survive—for Cara's sake. I'd find a way to escape.

CHAPTER 7

~ Asher ~

The human stabbed me.

The thought made me grin as I left her in the cavern, and the door sealed her inside.

No one had managed to wound me in over a hundred years, but somehow this human had pierced my shoulder with her simple blade. I thought of her confiscated dagger bobbing against my hip, and my pants grew tight.

I'd gone into her room blindly, I knew. None of the other humans had fought back, and I'd stupidly let my guard down. My brothers would have roared with laughter if I'd told them what had happened. Fuck, I'd been half-tempted to give the human her dagger back just so they could experience a surprise of their own.

My lips quirked into a mischievous smile. *Damned Halced, this human is refreshing.* Gorgeous, too, but plenty of monsters were stunning. It was more than that. She was...different.

I thought of the strange pain I'd felt when I'd touched her, then the undeniable force that was pulling me toward her. That was urging me to get close to her, to protect her. This female was more than just a human and it was going to be fucking fun finding out what.

I was still grinning when I entered the room I was after. Locke, Kade, and Darian stood before the magicked part of the wall that looked into the cavern I'd just been in, their gazes fixed on the human in white. The window was formed by magic, so the human wouldn't be able to see us, but we had a clear view. And it did *not* disappoint.

"Something amusing you, Ash?" Darian drawled.

Clearing my throat, I took up my position near two wooden levers that jutted out of the wall. "Yeah, you three actin' like monster pups fawning over that human."

Kade growled and didn't glance my way. "I'm not fawning. The human will turn soon."

I peered at the human who was busy dodging rocks that were raining down on her at a steady rate. Her face was contorted into a determined expression that I was finding way too appealing. I admired the speed at which she jumped and twirled around the falling bits of stone, her gauzy white dress rippling as she moved as if she were dancing to music only she could hear. None of the other humans had moved like that.

"Did she search for the door?" I asked.

"Briefly. She was smart enough to move on quickly," Locke said, his intense gaze tracking the human across the sand. Locke hadn't been this interested in anyone for over a century, and his curiosity about the human further fueled my own.

"Looks like our lovely little human might have some secrets," Darian mused. "She's certainly more prepared than the other chosen."

A rock the size of my head plummeted from the ceiling, and the human rolled out of the way just before it could crush her skull. Hysterical laughter spilled from her, unsettling me. Blood trickled down her lip, and sweat plastered her wild red hair to her scalp. She wiped her forehead with the back of her hand and sprang up in time to avoid another huge rock. *Too close. Change already*, I willed her.

I gripped one of the wooden levers that jutted from the wall.

"Be ready," Locke said.

"Always am," I said, then grinned at the memory of the human stabbing me. *Mostly.*

The human continued to dodge the rocks, but it was only a matter of time before one would hit her, her exhaustion slowing her pace. I pulled the first lever down, and the rocks stopped falling, but I didn't give her a reprieve.

Moving my hand to the other lever, I pushed it up.

The human's chest heaved, and she bent to rest her hands on her knees, but she looked up as a cracking sound vibrated down the cavern walls and dust plumed in the air.

"Seriously?" she yelled into the space, and Darian huffed a laugh.

The stone ceiling descended slowly but steadily toward her, the huge slab of rock reaching across the entire space, leaving no room for her to escape.

Time to show us your true face, Sharachi.

She raced around the cavern, running her hands along the walls, searching for the hidden door. When she found nothing, she dropped to her knees and thrust her hands downward, digging into the sand.

"No one's done that before," Darian commented, and Kade grunted in agreement.

The rocky ceiling was halfway down the cavern wall when she must have found it—the iron floor pocketed with trap doors that filtered away the falling rocks. It was specifically designed to sense the material of a rock and let it fall into the space below the cavern.

She cursed as she scraped her fingers along the iron.

I narrowed my eyes and found my usual smile falling as I watched her. My hand gripped the lever tighter. *Just turn already.*

But she remained the same. Her ears rounded, her skin lightly kissed by the sun, and her soft flesh as fragile as ever.

Human.

"Fuck. She's not going to change," Kade growled.

"Ash, put her out of her misery," Locke said, his black eyes glancing at the lever. His words were detached, but the claws starting to peek from his fingertips betrayed his concern.

I watched the human for a moment longer before heaving a sigh. "Fine. Really thought she'd change with this test though."

I began to pull the lever back down but frowned when it stuck halfway. *What the fuck?*

Darian smirked and arched a silver brow. "Having trouble?"

"Something's not right," I said peering at the level, then I turned to flash Darian a toothy smile. "It usually goes down as quickly as you do when we spar."

Darian tipped his head back with a snort. "Shall we test that theory?"

"How about we free the poor girl first, and then you can both piss off to the training cavern," Kade rumbled.

I pulled with more force, but it still didn't move.

"Get it to stop now," said Locke, his lethal command cracking through the air.

"Tryin' here," I said as I pulled the lever...right off the fucking wall. *Damn it, I had a feeling that would happen.*

Locke rounded on me, his eyes pure onyx black. "What the fuck did you do?"

Smiling sheepishly, I tossed the broken lever across the room. "Well, let's hope that did the trick."

Turning, I peered into the cavern. The human's fingers tore frantically at the iron now, and red blood flicked from her cut fingers onto the sand. The rocky ceiling was now only six feet above her head and still moving toward her. The constant sound of rock scraping against rock grated on my ears, and I clenched my jaw.

Reaching my hand down, I felt for the stub of the lever inside the wall. My fingers brushed over jagged pieces, but there was nothing to hold onto. *Who the fuck designed this thing?*

"I can't stop it," I said, feeling the impact of my words. The human would be crushed and she would die, all because some idiot made the lever out of wood rather than iron or steel. She was only a human, but the thought bothered me more than I was comfortable admitting.

As if someone had just shot me with a poison-tipped arrow, pain erupted in my chest, a matching pain to when I'd touched the human's arm, and my body tensed.

"Fix this, Ash," Kade growled. "The Taratun council won't be happy if we lose one."

"Fuck the Taratun," I retorted as the pain intensified, and I rubbed my chest with my palm.

The human was on her back in the sand now, her long red hair curling above her head and a single tear rolling down her cheek. The rocky ceiling continued toward her, only inches away from her body.

Uncontrolled rage waved from Locke, unlike anything I'd felt from him in years. He glared at me, and then he was gone from the room.

I grit my teeth. *Like absolute fuck am I going to let this happen.* There was something about this human. Something was pulling me toward her, and I wasn't about to let her die.

Taking a run up, I launched myself at the wall, crashing into it. An ear-piercing crack sounded as the rock crumpled beneath my force, the broken stone falling to my feet, creating an opening into the cavern. I eyed the thick slab of rocky ceiling that was being lowered by numerous iron chains. I'd pull the slab upward with sheer brute force if I had to. Squatting, I went to grab the edge of the rocky ceiling, but my mouth fell open in surprise as my fingers raked through...

Sand?

A wave of sand rushed downward as the rocky ceiling was transformed into the harmless grainy substance. It fell on the woman, coating her whole body, and she coughed, creating a little cloud of sand and dust in the air.

Locke burst through the door that had reformed on the other side of the cavern, his face the picture of wrath, but he stopped abruptly when he took in the carpet of sand, his shocked expression mimicking mine.

"Did she just...turn that rock into fucking sand?" Kade asked, his brows lowered.

I stared, not bothering to answer him. It was only then I realized the pain had disappeared from my chest. *What the?*

"What in the name of the Devil Enzal is this woman?" Darian said, his posture still relaxed despite what we'd just witnessed.

An odd smile formed on my face. "She's fucking trouble, that's what."

· · · · ● · ● · · ·

~ Raine ~

Sand was in my eyes, nose, and mouth, and I rolled to my side and began coughing violently. Rubbing at my face, I tried to get it off me, but I could feel the small grains still clinging between my breasts and scratching against my thighs when I moved. *Shit.* I couldn't worry about that now. I was *alive.*

Every thud of my heart echoed in my ears, and I kept picturing the slab of rock coming toward me, steadily falling until it was about to flatten me. I'd been sure I was about to die. My body was going to be crushed, and there was nothing I could do.

But just as the rocky ceiling touched my bloody fingertips, a strange energy had swirled in me, clouding my vision, and then the ceiling had disappeared. Turned to sand. Like the rocky ceiling had never been there at all. *Goddess, what happened?*

The horned monster, A-Two, stood just beyond a newly created opening in the cavern wall, his violet eyes watching me from across the space. At first, I could have sworn concern was twisting his expression, but now he had a crooked, amused smile plastered to his face. The asshole probably enjoyed the whole show.

Locke had broken through the door, which was visible again on the other side of the cavern, his face more terrifying than I'd ever seen it. Whatever had just happened, he wasn't happy about it.

I coughed again, my already raspy throat now as dry as paper. Struggling to swallow, I forced myself to my knees, then to my feet.

I couldn't stop shaking. I blinked furiously at the tears still leaking from my eyes and clenched my hands together, but it didn't help.

Locke stalked toward me. As he stopped in front of me, his gaze lingered on my bloody fingers before fixing on my face. I didn't move and stared into his unnatural onyx-colored eyes without fear. Exhaustion dragged at me, and I didn't have it in me to feel afraid. It was taking enough of my strength just to keep upright.

"Like what you see?" I said, my voice cold.

His face remained hard, but his lips quirked up slightly. "Of course, beautiful, it's always a pleasure to see you."

If I hadn't been so damn tired, I might have hit him, but thankfully, common sense prevailed and I left my poor battered fingers hanging by my sides. "Just take me to my room."

For all I knew they weren't done with me yet, but to my relief, he nodded and gestured to the open doorway. I tried to swallow again and took wobbly steps toward it, feeling A-Two's gaze on my back the whole way.

It was slow going as Locke and I trudged back to my room. My body refused to quit shaking, and I wasn't sure if the exhaustion I was feeling was just from the physical ordeal I'd had. Maybe A-Two was right, and I was turning into something. Something *wrong*.

Locke walked ahead of me, but I could tell he was keeping a slow pace for my sake. When we reached my room, I walked straight to the pitcher of pink liquid and downed the contents.

All right, fine, half the liquid spilled straight onto my chest, but I was beyond caring. And if it was poison, hell, it'd be a better way to go than being crushed to death or dying from thirst. Assuming it was a poison that killed me instantly.

When I looked up, Locke was still watching from the doorway, his gaze as intense as it had been since he'd entered the cavern. He eyed the empty pitcher, and I couldn't read his expression.

"If it's poison, I hope you put the good kind in there," I said, hoping he'd at least give me some indication as to whether I'd just doomed myself.

His head tipped to the side. "Good kind?"

"Yeah, where you die instantly. That'd be way better than the ones that cause excruciating pain for a full day before you die. That would suck."

"Huh," was all he said in response.

Right. Because of course the gorgeous monster would give you the nice poison, Raine.

I sighed and slumped onto the bed, turning away from the doorway.

There was a moment of silence, and then the door creaked shut, and I knew I was alone.

CHAPTER 8

~ Locke ~

I left the human's room, my face a mask of stone as I stalked down the tunnel, firelight flickering on the walls.

Fucking Halced. The human had nearly died. I didn't even know why the thought agitated me. She was only a human. Or was she? I remembered the pain that had pierced my chest when the stone slab had been about to crush her. The same pain I'd felt when we'd come back through the portal after the selection. I knew now that the human had done something to me. *It wasn't the portal.*

The thought of her infecting me with some kind of magic should have infuriated me more, but instead, my curiosity only grew. This human was the most interesting thing to happen to me and my brothers in a long time, and I wasn't about to let her go.

You won't be able to keep her forever. I grunted in frustration at the thought. Our curse was already turning her into something deadly, and I had to find out what. No monster I'd heard of could turn rock to sand. If my brothers and I didn't figure it out soon, we'd have to hand her over to the Taratun council.

Rolling my shoulders, I felt the weight lift from my back as my wings disappeared, my claws retracting back into my fingertips. I didn't need my father knowing anything was off.

I should have been on my way to the training room to burn off some of the anger and frustration pent up inside me, but I couldn't avoid seeing him. I'd already delayed my visit in favor of watching the human's second trial. Fuck, if we couldn't figure out what she was, I had no doubt it would be my father who would be tasked to extract her secrets. A low growl tore from between my lips, and my scowl deepened at the thought.

I ground my jaw as I wove through the tunnels to the lowest depths of the mountain. Gradually, the torches on the walls dimmed until it was almost black, and a bloodcurdling screech warped the air, a sign that I was close.

I passed huge iron doors, twice the size and thickness of those of my own room and marred with deep lines of scratches carved by the creatures locked inside.

One of the creatures howled and slammed into the door on my right, denting the iron from within, but I didn't pause and strode straight to my father's lab. To *Warrick's* lab. I didn't often call him *Father.* He didn't deserve the title.

Set up in a wide cavern, the walls of Warrick's lab were lined with thin wooden shelves holding the vials of blood and specimens he had collected over the years. I wrinkled my nose at the scent of monster blood, sulfur, and decay permeating the air.

Warrick's tall frame craned over the monster carcass sprawled on the stone table in the middle of the room. The creature was hard to distinguish with its body carved open, the contents of its stomach removed, but the top of its head was still intact, the long horns of the chimera reaching longer than the stone slab. I looked away in disgust and guilt from the monster Asher, Kade, and I had captured mere nights ago.

The monster wasn't like the rest of us. It was an outlier—an animal warped by the magic of the curse. Only humans used to be affected, but over the past decade, batches of animals had started turning as well. But unlike turned humans, animals had no conscience or remorse and seemed to have the sole goal to destroy other monsters. It was bad enough that we were still at war with the fae, but now we had this to worry about. And in the past year, the appearances of the outliers were increasing. The magic of the curse was changing, and no one knew why.

I knew I shouldn't feel guilty about bringing the monsters to Warrick. The creatures had to die, or else they'd slaughter countless citizens of Katakin, but my father wasn't known for killing his subjects quickly. No animal deserved that, whether it had been turned into an abomination or not.

"He called for you hours ago," hissed my father's assistant, a green-skinned goblin with gangly limbs, pointed ears, and a bloodied apron tied to his bulbous body. He'd been standing near a movable table filled with surgical tools, but he stepped over to stand before me and planted a hand on his hip.

I glowered at the goblin, letting him feel the full impact of the anger that was still pent up inside me from the encounter with the red-haired human.

The goblin stared back at me with a fanged smile, but after a moment, his shoulders curved inward, his body instinctively submitting, cowed by my dominance. Despite this, his smile grew as if the simple fact of knowing he got under my skin made him happy.

If my father ever found a cure for this damned curse and made us mortal again, the goblin would be the first one I'd get rid of. For now, I had to play nice.

"That's quite all right, Gosren. I'm sure my son had more important things to do," said my father sharply, peering up from his work.

My gaze roved over Warrick's appearance. He likely hadn't left this part of the mountain since we'd delivered the chimera, but his sleek black hair was combed neatly back, his red coat impeccable despite the black blood smeared on his apron. Warrick's bloodshot eyes fixed on me, and he faked a smile. "I trust all is going well with the trials?"

My face was neutral but my shoulders tensed, betraying my displeasure at being forced to be a part of the trials. "As well as can be expected."

"I've heard over half the humans are now in their monster forms and are being inducted by the Taratun. Your mother tells me the new vampire looks promising."

I resisted the urge to curl my lip. "The new vamp isn't my problem."

Warrick raised a brow, his suggestive look making my anger simmer. "You're quite right. She's not a problem, she's an *opportunity.* It's time you took your place as alpha of our house. It would look good if you took her as your mate."

I tried to contain my fury, but the thought of me standing beside my father as alpha of the House of Nesarin—the high house of vampires—with a vampire mate on my arm had a low hiss releasing from my lips. "There are others more suited to the position. I don't want to be part of your house."

"Those pretenders don't have the power you do. If you applied yourself, you could..." He shook his head in frustration and sneered. "I've allowed you to play your games and waste your time with those monsters you call your 'brothers,' even though they aren't your vampire kin, but enough is enough. Leave them to finish the trials. It's time for you to focus on more important matters."

Claws shot from my fingertips, and I fought back the urge to sink my fangs into flesh. "I will *not* leave Kade and the others." Blinking, I took a deep breath, surprised by my own sudden outburst. I hated Warrick—all I'd ever been to him was another experiment—but his comment wasn't anything new. Warrick insulted Kade and the others often, and while it angered me, it never made me feel like ripping my father's head off.

The trials. The human. I didn't let my realization show on my face. Just a week ago, I'd been grumbling about the fact we'd been assigned to carry out the trials. Now I didn't want to give them up. If I left my brothers to the trials, I'd also be leaving the human girl. Something I was not prepared to do. That human was a mystery, and I intended to find out everything about her without letting Warrick dissect her.

Even at this moment, it was almost as if I could smell...

My gaze flicked to the glass vials of blood lining the cavern. Most of the vials were an inky black, filled with monster blood, but a few of the samples were taken from the humans before they turned.

The samples of blood dried out over the years, but a small section of the wall contained the fresh samples from the latest round of humans. My nostrils flared when I spotted the red vials, and my gaze narrowed as I identified the two that contained *her* blood. Her irresistible scent found its way to me, tempting me and fueling the hunger deep inside me. Saliva dripped down my fangs, but I kept my lips clamped together.

Warrick was visiting the humans every night to take samples and analyze their blood during the change. He believed the secrets in their blood formed part of the key to unlocking how to break the curse. But the thought of him with the humans while they were unconscious made me sick. Fuck, I hoped her blood didn't smell as delicious to him as it did to me.

I forced my attention back to him. "You didn't ask me here to talk. What do you need?" I knew if Warrick was serious about forcing me to take my place as alpha of the House of Nesarin, he wouldn't be standing there saying idle threats. The old fool still hoped I'd take my place willingly. I would be glad to disappoint him. I wanted nothing to do with that house of horrors.

His mouth widened to a cold smile, and an eager spark lit up his eyes. "I need more subjects."

"We found you the chimera only a week ago," I said with a frown.

His long fingers placed the bloodied scalpel on the table, and he hummed a happy little tune as he gestured to the mutilated body before him, like he was proud of his work.

"As you can see, it didn't last long. I can only work as fast as the supply."

My gaze darkened, guilt for the creatures rising again to the surface. "It's not right. Doing this to them."

He cocked his head, eyeing me quizzically. "Would you rather we left them out there to ravage the city? Kill our citizens?"

"If we kept them locked up—"

"There aren't enough rooms in this mountain to keep them all here indefinitely. And if they got out, the consequences would be dire. We need to find a cure, and this is the way to make that happen."

"You can't cure a curse," I said bitterly. "You've searched for nearly two centuries. Only the queen could break the curse, and no one's seen her since she disappeared through that portal two hundred years ago."

"Well, yes, fae magic is a fickle thing, but I believe anything can be cured. There must be a way to force our bodies to physically change back, and I will find it. To do that, I need to study these new monsters. These animals." His expression became serious. "Don't forget my position on the council is the only reason you and your...*friends* are able to stay together. Having four monsters of different types together is unnatural, and there are many who detest the idea. It confuses the newbloods."

I clenched and unclenched my fist at my side, but I didn't let him goad me into an argument. "We're busy with the trials. Zacal's team is on city patrol tonight. Why not get them to bring you something?"

Before I took a breath, Warrick was before me, his face close to mine and his penetrating glare boring into me. Despite being three decades older than me, the male appeared only five years older, with age lines crinkling around his eyes. "The Taratun council lets me operate down here because I get rid of the monsters we can't control. So far, no one on the council has asked questions, but after all these years, there are some who want the curse to remain. They can't find out what I'm trying to do. Zacal won't be able to keep his mouth shut."

My eye twitched. I could likely take out my father with my vampire body if I wanted—I was one of the few monsters who stood a chance against him—but I wasn't an animal. *If he finds a cure, we could be human again*, I reminded myself. Wanting to find a cure was the only thing my father and I agreed on. He was our only hope, and he knew it. I set my jaw and gave a small nod. "Fine. I'll be back in a few hours. You'd better be ready."

His face broke into a cruel smile, the eagerness returning to his eyes. "Gosren and I will be waiting."

CHAPTER 9

~ Locke ~

I stalked into the common room my brothers and I shared, slamming the door behind me, and heading straight for the bottle of alcohol on the high table tucked against the wall. Pouring the clear liquid into a goblet, I lifted the steel cup to my lips. Alcohol did little for me in this cursed monster body, not unless I downed a significant quantity, but I savored the burn as the liquid slid down my throat.

"What did he want?" Kade asked. His alert gaze had been tracking me since I'd entered the room. He finished polishing his long swords and slid them into his leather scabbards.

"Nothing good by the looks of it," Darian said as he sipped from his own goblet.

"More subjects," I said darkly. I poured another goblet, not caring when some of the liquid spilled onto the table.

"That vampire goes through bodies faster than Asher and Darian go through females," Kade growled, his body stilling.

"Hasn't it only been a week?" Darian questioned. "He can't need more already. What the devil is he doing with them?"

You don't want to know. I downed the alcohol from my second goblet and slammed the cup onto the table, making the wood shake from the force, then I turned to the others. "I'm going hunting."

Kade stood, the wood of the settee creaking at the removal of his weight. "We'll all go."

"No. It's Darian's trial next. We agreed we'd each carry out a trial, and I don't know how long I'll be gone. Someone should also stay to watch in case anything goes awry while Darian's with the humans."

"I'd say I'm sad to be missing the fun, but these humans are rather entertaining," Darian said with a gleam in his eye.

Kade's brow creased, and he folded his thick arms over his chest. "Asher can stay with Darian. He's busy watching over the repairs of the mechanisms and levers at the stone cavern anyway. I'll join you."

I gave a curt nod, grateful to have him with me to watch my back. "Zacal's team are on foot patrol tonight. We'll have to stay out of their way. Don't want this taking longer than it needs to." Bringing Kade with me while Zacal was out wasn't the best idea, but we'd keep far from them.

"Will Warrick be ready for us when we return?"

I strode to the shelf of weapons and strapped on another belt that I proceeded to fill with steel. "He's looking forward to it," I said as I slid another dagger onto my hip.

Kade grunted and strapped his long swords to his back before joining me at the weapons shelf.

I ground my teeth. *This better be fucking worth it.* "Don't forget the rope."

• • • • • • • • • •

Kade and I were silent as we wound down one of the hidden staircases that led to Katakin City beyond the mountain. We moved swiftly in the pitch dark, not bothering to bring a torch, and using our night vision to guide us down the steps. Every so often my shoulder would brush against the fabric of Kade's shirt as we moved in the narrow space.

We reached the base of the mountain a while later and stepped into the moonlight. I breathed in deeply, taking in the crisp air and scents of pine and vegetation among the sulfur, and the tightness in my chest loosened. The walls of the mountain always reminded me of my father's grip, tightening around me, and even though at this very moment I was off to do his bidding, it still felt freeing to be outside.

Kade's gaze roved around the darkened clearing where we'd emerged. Lifting his nose, he scented the air, his wolf sense of smell only slightly keener than my vampire senses. Seemingly satisfied that we were alone, he turned to me and spoke. "Zacal's team might be hotheaded, but they're not incompetent. His wolves will scent our whereabouts if we enter the city. It will be hard to keep our movements a secret."

I cracked the bones in my neck and flexed my back before pulling my sword from the scabbard at my side. "We'll keep to the forest and only enter the outskirts of the city if we have to. If we're fast enough, we'll be gone before we're detected."

"Might be hard to do if the outlier runs into a populated area," Kade reasoned. "Not to mention we could easily be spotted by the guard towers."

My face remained passive. "I'll come up with something if we're seen by the gargoyles in the towers. As for Zacal...we'll deal with him and his wolves if we have to." Warrick was right to suggest that Zacal wouldn't be able to keep his mouth shut about the experiments on the outliers. The wolf alpha of the House of Worzel was as untrustworthy as they came, and he still had it out for Kade. We didn't need Zacal finding us out there. He was only such a cocky bastard because Kade wouldn't fight back. While I understood why sometimes I wished Kade would give just enough to remind the male to leave him the fuck alone. To remind him that the only reason he had the position as alpha was because Kade stepped down.

Kade was quiet, his face sullen, and I knew he was thinking about his family. He wouldn't fight Zacal. I wished he'd stop punishing himself, but nothing I said or did could have taken away his pain.

"We'll stay out of the city," I stated again, placing my hand on his shoulder.

· · · ● · ● ● · · ·

It didn't take long before we'd reached a stretch of forest that ended a hundred yards before the edge of the northern district of the city. The lively music and rowdy laughter of monsters walking the streets filled my sensitive ears, even from out here. I stopped in the shadow of a tall pine tree and waited, staring out at the glow of blue light coming from the lanterns lining the cobbled city streets and falling on the tall brick buildings crammed together. If there was something out there, the sounds of the busiest side of the city would draw it out.

Kade took up a similar stance a few yards away, and he sniffed the air. His ears morphed, becoming pointed, and they twitched as he assessed the sounds around him, but the rest of his body remained human. He wouldn't change completely unless he had to. Releasing his wolf wasn't the best way to bring in an outlier if we wanted it to still be breathing.

An hour passed with nothing but the usual brawls spilling from taverns and altercations on the streets that were soon broken up. No signs of any unusual activity.

I was about to signal to Kade and motion for us to move to a different position further around the city when a thunderous roar shattered through the brick buildings, making the ground tremble. The laughter in the city was replaced by screams and bellows, and the thud of footsteps filled my ears as monsters ran to take shelter indoors.

Kade's gaze shot to mine, but I shook my head. *Not yet.* The outlier sounded too far into the city. Zacal's team would have to deal with it.

An answering roar came from further south of the city, and I frowned. *Another outlier. How the fuck are they getting so far into the city?* My fangs peeked from between my lips, and my wings burst from my back as my body instinctively started to react to the challenge these new threats presented.

Kade heard the third outlier just before I did, his hands flying to the hilts of his swords, drawing the blades.

I turned, lifting my sword as a great beast barreled through the forest, its wide body ripping branches from the trees as if they were nothing but twigs in its way. The creature was as tall as a horse and four times as wide, the largest outlier I'd seen so far. *There's a third one.* The fact the monster had stayed undetected until it was this close to us irked me, but I had no time to dwell on it now.

The creature's three glowing red eyes slid to Kade and then fixed on me, clearly deciding I would be its first victim. Not that I would let that happen.

Swinging in my direction as it ran, its bulging muscles propelled its black body forward with unnatural speed, even by monster standards. Before it could reach me, I jumped into the air and over the creature's body, using my wings to gain extra height. A crack rang out as the beast impacted with the pine I'd previously been standing in front of, and the tree toppled to the ground with a thud.

I dropped back to the ground as the creature shook its head and turned, saliva dripping from its long, bared fangs. Scraggly black fur covered the demon dog's thick body, and oddly shaped muscles protruded from its arms, as if the muscles were too big for its skin. *A barghest.* I'd never seen a demon dog in the flesh before, but I recognized it from one of the books I had stashed in my room.

The outlier pulled its pointed ears back as it roared, sending spittle flying, and I winced at the deafening sound. A single answering roar came from within the city, and I knew that meant Zacal and his wolves must have managed to take down one of the outliers. We were running out of time.

Steel glinted as Kade growled and launched at the creature from the side, his swords cutting through the air. In a whirl of movement, the barghest leaped, meeting Kade before he struck. The creature smashed its huge head into Kade's chest, sending him flying backward into the forest.

Two knives shot out from my hands, sinking into the flesh of the outlier's hind legs while it was in midair. When the creature landed, I was waiting. My sword sliced a stripe behind the creature's muscular shoulders in one smooth motion.

The creature turned its head, its huge, gnashing jaws snapping onto my blade and sending it careening out of my grasp. Black blood dripped from where the blade had cut the monster's mouth, but it didn't seem to care.

The outlier stared at me and roared again, uncontrolled rage in its glowing red eyes. Its huge, fleshy nostrils flared, and it snorted as Kade appeared again with hardly a scratch on him.

We faced off the creature, each of us to one side. "Would you fucking put this thing to sleep already?" Kade said. He was still mostly human, but sharp fangs peeked from his mouth and claws had extended from his fingertips.

"I need to get closer to it. Get the rope ready," I responded.

The outlier eyed the both of us, its ears flicking as if it was listening to what we were saying but not understanding the words. It snarled in Kade's direction as Kade sheathed his swords and pulled the coiled rope from where it was clipped to his side. "Let's get this done."

I didn't need any encouragement. The moment the creature lunged at me again, I flapped my wings and launched into the air, a gray powder already in my hand. Blowing the powder into the beast's face, I landed on its back as Kade lassoed the monster and tightened the rope, pulling its front legs together. I jumped from the creature's back as it thudded to the ground. The beast sneezed and strained against its binds, trying to stand.

Kade yanked on the rope, pulling it tight against the beast's legs, a growl tearing from his own throat at the effort. Opening its mouth, the creature went to let out another roar, but I blew another handful of powder in its face, and it snapped its mouth shut.

Its nostrils flared again before its eyes shuttered, and it collapsed on the ground with a small whine. Kade and I watched and waited until the creature's breathing steadied and we were sure it wasn't a threat.

"That's the biggest one we've seen yet," Kade said as we neared the monster. "What do you think it used to be?"

"No fucking idea." I eyed the creature's form right down to its bushy tail, the ends brittle and singed as if it had been dipped in fire. It could have been a rabbit for all we knew. The only thing that was clear was that it wasn't human. There was only hatred in those red eyes, no recognition.

Kade cursed and ran a hand through his hair. "What the hell is happening?"

He said it out loud, but I knew he didn't expect me to answer. Living in this monster hellhole had never been easy, but these outliers were bringing a whole new meaning to the word *monster*. When humans turned, they had elements of humanity—a conscience, remorse, guilt, and most importantly, control over their own bodies. They were able to fit in with society and learn to control their monstrous urges. If they stepped out of line, they knew the consequences were dire.

But these...outliers, they seemed to want nothing but to tear apart anyone they came into contact with. They couldn't be reasoned with. Whatever magic the queen had used to make the curse that turned us all into monsters, something was twisting it. Who the fuck knew what we were going to do when even our own livestock started turning into those creatures.

My gaze lifted to further south, where the majority of our cattle was under heavy guard just outside the city. It was a wonder that none of those animals hadn't yet turned, or at least, not to our knowledge. So far, it seemed to only be the wild animals from the forest that were being affected. *Why?* It was the question that haunted me.

"We have to hope Warrick will pull through." I hated the words that came out of my mouth, but they were true. My father was the only one studying the outliers. The others on the council still refused to admit the creatures were a threat. *Ignorant bastards.*

A strange sinking feeling dropped in my gut as I thought about the fiery human who would soon be having her next trial with Darian. *What if she is different because the curse is warping her into some perversion of a monster? What if she's stripped of her humanity during the change?* I knew exactly what would happen. My father would want to study her. My fist clenched.

Dropping down, I crouched next to the barghest, ignoring the unsavory scents of decay and sweat coating the folds under its belly.

A chorus of frantic wolf howls sounded from within the city, but I ignored them.

"Zacal's team has slain the other outliers," Kade growled.

"Help me roll it over," I said, placing my hands under the creature's body. "Let's get it tied properly. We have to move."

Kade grunted and squatted beside me.

CHAPTER 10

~ Raine ~

I groaned as I awoke, exhaustion making it feel as though my limbs were pinned to the bed. Soon after Locke had left my room, I'd fallen into a fitful sleep, but now the truth of what had happened finally sank in.

The monsters tried to crush me to death. An unexpected pang of hurt rippled through me. *What did you think they were going to do to you? They're monsters.*

I squeezed my eyes shut but then forced them open again. I couldn't let them break me. I couldn't let *this* break me. Whatever had happened to turn the rocky slab into sand, it was over, and I had to be grateful. All that mattered was me finding a way to escape these monsters and save Cara. *Just wait for your moment, then get the fuck outta there.*

Flexing my fingers, I winced at the pain of my cuts. *That'll slow me down.* Frowning, I stretched out my right arm. It was throbbing again, another red dot on the inner crease, and my head was light, but otherwise, I was fine. I still had no idea what they were doing to me while I slept, but at this point, a part of me wondered if it was better not to know.

An uncomfortable burning in my belly was what finally made me sit up. *Note to self: don't down a pitcher of liquid before going to sleep.* I swung my feet to the floor with the plan to disappear into the washroom, when there was a knock on my door.

I stood as the door opened, my muscles instinctively tightening and my hands curling into fists.

"Do you always greet your visitors with such hostility?" said a melodic masculine voice.

I gaped at the monster standing in the doorway. Glossy silver hair was pulled back from his flawless, smooth face, and defined muscle covered his bare chest, ending in a *V* above loose-fitting silver trousers. My brows lowered when I realized his feet were bare, and I couldn't see a weapon. I lifted my gaze back to his face.

Crystal-blue eyes framed by long lashes were watching me curiously, and his thin lips pulled into a sensual smile. Locke had more of a dark, lethal beauty, and A-Two had masculine charm, but this monster was the most elegant of the four. A regal expression fixed on his perfect face.

It took me a moment to work out he was the fourth monster, the cloaked one who'd been present during the

Night of the Offering. I wondered why he'd worn the cloak that night. *Probably because he thought he didn't look menacing enough. The villagers in the lineup might have volunteered for the offering if they'd seen this male's face.* A smirk threatened to twist my lips.

Asshole monster. Not man, I scolded myself. But it was an easy mistake to make. Aside from the monster's unusual height, he didn't have any of the blatant monster traits the others did. No claws or fangs. *Or a freaking tail.*

"And how would you have me greet you?" I said in mockery, finally answering his question.

His smile grew, his eyes sparkling. "Oh, we'll get to that in time. What's your name, lovely?"

My mouth popped open slightly. "My—what?"

"Your name. I'm not a barbarian like my brothers, and I'm sure you have one. Unless, of course, you want me to call you 'human'?"

For a moment, my lips didn't move, shock freezing them in place. None of the other monsters had asked me. Something about giving him my name felt so personal, but it definitely would be better than being called "human." I mean, sure, I'd been calling him A-Three, but he didn't need to know that.

"Raine," I finally said.

"R-ai-ne." He said my name as if he was rolling it over on his tongue and tasting it. "Now, that is delightful."

I swallowed, trying to ignore the strange fluttering in my stomach. "And yours?" I asked. It seemed only fair to get a name in return, though I doubted he would tell me.

"Darian," he said without hesitation, surprising me. "But you can call me Dar."

Darian. I nodded. I wasn't about to call him by a nickname like we were close friends.

"Well, it's my turn, Raine lovely. Ready?" he said and stepped to the side of the doorway, gesturing to the tunnel.

A burning sensation still pulled at my belly, and my gaze flicked to the door that led to the washroom. Turning back to the monster, I raised a brow. "No?"

"This test won't be as bad as the last one. Trust me," he said with a chuckle.

"Right, as if I'd trust you."

Like the other monsters, he did nothing but smile at my blunt tongue, and his lips parted to show glistening white teeth. "You're a smart one."

Something about his words sent a chill skittering down my spine.

His head tipped toward the doorway. "Let's go, lovely."

I hesitated a moment longer, then stepped into the tunnel. *I can hold it.* No point delaying the inevitable. *Just watch for your moment.*

• • • • • • • • • •

This cavern wasn't at all like the last one. The space was huge, easily ten times the size of the one the horned demon had taken me to. And unlike that cavern, this one wasn't empty. A huge mass of water spread across the floor like an underground lake. At the far end, water rushed down a rocky wall, sliding over large boulders that lay over one another and spraying into the lake. We stood in the shallows, the cool black water licking over my toes.

Instead of torches, thousands of amethyst crystals covered the top of the cavern, shining a dull purple over the water and making the black sparkle like the reflection of the night sky.

It was...breathtaking. *Maybe Darian's right and this won't be as bad as the last one.* I wanted to believe it. Hell, my throbbing fingers demanded it, but I knew better than to be so naive. There was something in the dammed ink-colored water, and unfortunately, I was about to find out what.

Mother Falia, I wish I had my dagger. I internally cursed A-Two for stealing it from me. Sure, I had stabbed him, but come on.

Darian reached down and pulled off his pants, throwing them near the door. *What the?* I turned my head, refusing to look at him. Refusing to look *down. What the hell is he doing?*

Before I could ask, he took a step further into the water, the black liquid rising just above his ankles. Then he turned back and held out his hand, his long, delicate fingers reaching toward me. "Come now, Raine. Let's have some fun."

I glared and ignored his hand. "I'm not going in there."

He left his hand outstretched. "Not a fan of water?"

In fact, I loved water. I enjoyed swimming in the beaches around the island whenever I had a spare moment. We often needed the fish, and the times when I was weightless in the water were the only ones when I felt like my guilt about Cara wasn't crushing me.

I eyed the lake suspiciously. "It's not the water I'm wary of. Let me guess, as soon as I move, giant tentacles are going to launch from the depths and drag me under?"

He laughed, and the carefree sound vibrated in my bones. My gaze almost slid down his body, but I forced myself to keep staring at his face.

"Such dark expectations. I promise you, there's no one here besides us. We're going in there whether you like it or not. It's up to you whether you walk in by yourself or I grab you and take you with me." His lips twitched upward into an impish smile, and I narrowed my eyes in challenge. Unconsciously, my gaze trailed to his bare, muscular chest, and I snapped my attention back to his face.

Focus, Raine. I eyed his hand again. I didn't doubt I would be forced into the water. Darian might not have had any obvious monster traits, but the power that pulsed from him still made my heart race. But if I had to go, I'd do it on my terms. I had some dignity.

Reluctantly, I placed my hand onto his. As our palms touched, energy zapped up my fingers, rushing up my arms. I gasped as agony seared through me, like my very blood was on fire, sizzling beneath my skin. It was exactly as it had felt when I'd come through the portal and when A-Two had touched me.

"What did you do?" I accused, pulling my hand back. Like it had with A-Two, the pain abruptly disappeared, and I sucked in a shuddering breath.

Darian blinked slowly, and his brow creased. "Did yo—" He stopped himself and stretched his fingers before clenching his fist and turning toward the water. "Follow me," he said, all humor gone from his voice. "Don't make me drag you in."

An uneasy feeling wiggled inside me. Either he didn't mean to zap me with his magic, or something was going on that he wasn't telling me about.

I sighed heavily. Since I'd arrived, I'd been bombarded with secrets and had the attention of way too many sexy asshole monsters. *Cara probably went through all of this. You'll find her.* I didn't remind myself that Cara was likely dead. *Was she crushed to death?* I shook the thought away.

Darian obviously had no doubt I would follow him into the water, as by now he was halfway across the lake and the water reached up to his thighs. Without so much as a look in my direction, he dived, disappearing into the inky darkness.

I waited for him to reappear, but moments passed, and not even a ripple showed on the surface. I chewed the inside of my cheek and waited for some horrible monster to spring from the dark depths of the water. Darian may have said nothing was in there besides us, but as if I'd believed him.

Peering behind me, I was surprised to find the door to the cavern remained open. A stupid smile sprang to my face. There it was. My chance to escape. I turned, ready to leg it out of there, when a bewitching tune sang to me over the water.

I stilled and tilted my head to one side. The notes were light and seductively smooth as they rose and fell, a captivating melody that wrapped around me filling my senses. Every thought emptied out of my mind as I became enchanted by the music. *You need to*—I couldn't remember. Whatever I had been about to do became a forgotten memory as note after note captured me. My body warmed, tingles spreading from the tips of my fingers to my toes.

The music grew louder, and an intense longing began to lead me deeper into the water, as if I was a boat being pulled by a strong current, bobbing along the waves.

It felt as though no time had passed when I found the cool water up to my waist, splashing at my arms and swirling around me as if it had a mind of its own. And then I saw him.

His torso reached above the water, every chiseled muscle gleaming under the purple lights from above. His silver hair had escaped from his ponytail and waved down his neck, and blue eyes that glittered like sapphires fixed on me.

His mouth was open, and his song continued to fill the air, notes flowing from his perfect lips, lips that I had to have on mine. Because I was *his*. And *only* his. The words echoed through every part of me, filling me with a lightness I relished. I wanted him to consume me, devour me. Nothing else mattered except that I had to get to him.

As if I had wished it true, suddenly he was before me. I had no idea how I'd gotten to him so fast, but I didn't care. Smiling, I traced my fingertips down the hard ridges of his achingly perfect chest.

A forgotten thought pressed against the edges of my mind, but I ignored it. How could I want to be thinking about anything else? A grin teased his lips as he sang to me, but then I was pressing my mouth to his neck, his skin cool on my lips, my tongue. He was sweet and salty all at the same time.

Water sprayed on me as a large, shimmering blue fishtail flicked out of the water and curled around my body, pulling me harder against him. I shivered as silky scales slipped across my back, sliding against my skin. A nagging thought pushed more incessantly at my mind, and this time, I pulled back with a frown. *There's something...*

My thought trailed off as two strong arms wrapped around me, and his body ground against mine. He pulled me deeper into the water, and I savored the feeling of his hands on my skin. But it wasn't enough. I had to have *more*. Heat grew in my core, and I squirmed, my need making me antsy.

Lifting me in the water, he cupped my ass, and I wrapped my legs around his torso. I writhed, desperate for more friction. His eyes grew hooded, and he dropped his mouth against the side of my head, his rich song taking me deeper into a blissful state.

My vision became a haze of purple, silver, and black, nothing but happiness filling me. "Please," I whispered, but he only continued to sing.

The faint rush of water sounded in my other ear, and I vaguely noticed the water spraying on the boulders to my left, droplets flying onto my face. I blinked once. There was something about that sound. I turned to the waterfall, hardly registering the water that rained from above. The niggling thought from before clawed at my mind, and my head began to ache.

Hands tightened on my body, and a moan escaped me as he nuzzled my ear. My head throbbed more intensely as a thought tried to break through. *There was something I had to... If I could just...* The pain in my head grew so bad I squeezed my eyes shut, and then a burning bloomed in my stomach. An aching, bursting, unbearable feeling that cut through the fog of my mind. I had to get it out. I *needed* to get it out. I needed to...

"I NEED TO PEE!" I screeched, my eyes snapping open. Startled arms released me, and I toppled backward, my head falling below the water before I had the sense to move my arms and rise again to the surface. I spluttered and sucked in a huge, gasping breath, one hand reaching down to rest on my aching abdomen.

Blinking, I peered around as if I was finally seeing clearly for the first time in a long while. An eerie silence filled the cavern, the only sound the rush of the water.

Darian was still before me, his ridiculously sculpted chest still bare. I stared at that chest as I struggled to understand what I'd just done. "Did I just... *Taste you*?" My mouth gaped open in horror.

I recoiled, moving backward in the water, and another thought came to me. "And do you have a freaking *fishtail*?"

He stared at me for a moment longer as if shocked by my outburst, but then he tipped his head back, and the bastard *laughed*. And it wasn't just ordinary laughter but the tears-coming-out-of-your-eyes kind of laughter.

I'm going to kill him.

I'd been tricked. *Violated.* Somehow entranced to think he was some sort of love god, and I was his, and we were perfect together, and... I didn't have time right now to kick his ass. Because I wasn't lying. I needed to relieve myself. I needed to pee *badly*. The sound of all the rushing water made me *desperate* to go. I was an idiot for trying to hold it. I was now convinced that the burning in my stomach was worse than any of the tortures the monsters had put me through.

I didn't wait for Darian. I'd have to deal with his violating hands later. Turning, I didn't even wait for him to finish laughing, I just raced out of there. I expected him to stop me at the door, but he only followed, his footsteps padding behind me. I vaguely wondered how he was able to lose his tail so quickly, but right now, I had bigger things to think about.

I retraced our steps back to my room with surprising accuracy. I never would have expected to have remembered the way back, but it seems when your body is in a desperate situation, it's amazing what it can accomplish.

I made it back in record time and slammed the door before Darian could follow me in. I mean, he could open the door, of course, but just the act of slamming a door in his face left me with a small sense of satisfaction.

Using the water closet was utter bliss. *Way more blissful than having my legs wrapped around...* Heat flooded me, and I clenched my legs together. *What would have happened if I hadn't needed to pee and broken myself out of the trance?*

I groaned, frustrated at myself. I'd been tortured three times since tumbling into this maddening world, and each time, I'd proved I was no match for these monsters. I was never going to be able to slip away and find Cara.

Striding back into the main room, I nibbled some crusty bread, and gulped down a cup of the pink liquid that had been replenished while I had been sleeping earlier.

When moments passed and Darian still didn't appear, I stripped out of my dress, laid it on the floor to dry, and crawled onto the cot. Then I threw the blanket over myself and pretended I could block out the world and the treacherous images of a muscled monster chest that kept appearing in my mind. *Monster assholes.*

CHAPTER II

~ Darian ~

"What the fuck was that, Dar?"

I padded to where my brothers stood before a rocky wall, leaving a trail of wet footprints in my wake.

"What was what?" I asked innocently, turning to look at Locke's hard expression.

"You know what," Kade growled. "You don't let the humans touch you. You sing enough to get them entranced and searching for you, but you don't let them touch you."

I shrugged nonchalantly. "Our lovely human wasn't changing, so I thought I'd give her a stronger dose."

"You entranced her so deeply she lost all sense of herself," Kade added.

My lips curled upward. "I just wanted to know..." I trailed off as I recalled the strange crackling energy I'd felt when the human had taken my hand. It had almost reminded me of... I shook my head, purging my mind of the thoughts that were impossible. It was obviously some weird malfunction of my own power. No point telling the others I was damaged. Still, I'd wanted to see what would happen if I touched her again. The strange sensation hadn't repeated when her tongue had slid up my neck. Nor when her legs had straddled me like—

Asher shoved my arm. "Stop grinning so hard. You look like an idiot."

"Jealous, brother?" I asked, my smile widening.

Asher laughed. "Do you blame me?"

"You wanted to know *what* exactly?" Locke said.

I glanced at Locke, and the lie came out easily. "If she could handle more, and if something would happen. She turned a rocky ceiling to sand last time. Who's to say what else she can do?"

All four of us were silent as tension filled the air.

"She broke free from my power today," I finally added, breaking the silence.

"She needed to pee," Asher commented pointedly with a smirk.

A smile teased my lips, but my expression remained thoughtful. "No one has ever broken free. Not just with my power. Breaking the power of any siren isn't heard of." I turned to look at the rocky wall, and as if on command, the wall shimmered and became clear, and then I could see out over the waterfall and across the span of water in the adjoining cavern.

Locke and the others stepped up beside me and followed my gaze over the water.

"How was the hunt?" I asked.

Locke exhaled sharply and his eyes darkened. "We captured a barghest. Warrick is satisfied for now."

"The beast was almost the size of a small house," Kade added. "This one better last him fucking longer than the chimera."

Locke continued to stare at the lake. "The outliers are becoming more common. There were three barghests tonight." Turning his head, he peered at me. "Anything out of the ordinary happen with the other humans?"

I shook my head. "Four more changed today. Three sirens with the power of song, and a banshee who almost burst my eardrums before I overpowered her. They were all shocked, but they still had their humanity, mostly."

"With the others that have already turned, that leaves two remaining humans in a mountain of monsters," Asher added, folding his arms across his chest.

"The only one who was different is Raine," I said, gesturing to the waterfall and the lake, though the human was back in her room. "The others succumbed to my song with hardly any effort."

Three pairs of eyes shot to me, and I didn't hide the ridiculous smile on my face.

"Raine?" Locke asked, and I didn't miss the irritation in his voice.

"The human," I said casually. "Her name's Raine."

My brothers continued to stare at me as if they couldn't believe what I was saying. I knew this would bother them. It was clear the human had us all curious, and the fact I knew more about her than they did had to be eating them alive.

"Next, he'll be saying he wants to claim her during the Week of Orash," Kade growled.

I arched a brow. I had no intention of fighting to claim one of the newly turned, but Raine was...special. The idea of her joining the House of Saceris—high house of the water monsters—annoyed me. I only hoped she didn't turn into any kind of water monster so there was no chance she could join my old house. She didn't belong with those self-conceited pretenders any more than I did. Being with the House of Saceris would stifle her spirit.

Would I fight to claim the lovely Raine if she turned into a water monster? There was something irresistible about her. Ever since she'd touched my palm, I couldn't stop picturing her beautiful face or her delectable body. And the feel of her tongue on my neck was—

"I'm up tomorrow," Kade said, pulling me from my thoughts. "Then we'll know what she is. No one has made it through the fourth test without changing."

CHAPTER 12

~ Raine ~

A fist banging on my door startled me awake. "Go away," I grumbled, my words slurred with sleep. It was hard to know how much time had passed in this forsaken place without sunlight to mark passing days, but weariness made it hard to move. *Are there days in hell? Or am I just enduring a single long night for eternity?*

The hinges on the door squeaking and the torches on the walls flaring to life alerted me to the fact someone had entered my room. I should have jumped out of bed, ready to face my intruder, but today it was as if all of my strength had been sapped away. They'd tried to kill me, toyed with me, and frankly, they could wait a few damn minutes.

"Time to go, Sharachi," said a deep voice.

Ah, A-Two. The bastard who'd tried to crush me. *Well, he can wait a little longer before putting me through another ordeal like that.* "A few more minutes," I mumbled. If he wanted to torture me, he'd have to get me out of bed first. I suspected the hard mattress was part of the torture, but honestly, it was similar to what I had at home. *Home.* It was funny thinking of the island and our village as that. After Cara had been taken, the island hadn't felt like home anymore, but I guessed that was what it was.

Heavy steps came closer to the bed, and the strange pull I felt when I was near the monster came to life, urging me to move closer to him. I cracked open an eye and peeked out at the figure towering over me.

An amused grin pulled at A-Two's mouth. "Look, I get it. If I had my way, I'd still be in bed as well. But the thing is, Kade hates waiting."

Kade? "Good for him." I shut my eyes again but sighed in resignation. Angering any monster did seem like a bad idea even if it was satisfying. I was about to lift my ass when my thin blanket was ripped from me.

I yelped and curled into a ball on my side. "What the hell!"

"Shit, sorry, I didn' realize you were, uh—" A-Two's gaze traveled from where he now spotted my white dress spread out on the floor and then back to me in only my panties.

"My dress was wet, asshole," I said, snatching the blanket back. I was about to wrap it around myself, but A-Two's heated gaze had me stilling, the blanket forgotten. His gaze slowly trailed to my breasts and belly before lifting again, a mischievous glint brightening his eyes.

My nipples hardened in response, my pulse quickening. Logically, I knew I should have been wanting to stab the monster, perhaps in the eye this time, but his gaze had my breath catching in my throat.

Just when I thought he was about to reach for me, he swallowed and blinked as if pulled from his own trance, though he didn't seem at all remorseful for his wandering gaze. "I'll wait outside. You'd better get dressed."

He started toward the door but stopped and turned back to me. "Or don't," he said with a wink and exited the room.

I cursed under my breath, hastily pulled on my dress, and rushed to use the water closet—I wasn't going to make *that* mistake again. After shoving a mouthful of bread into my mouth, I found the arrogant bastard waiting, his violet eyes glowing in the darkness. His gaze raked over my body in the dress. "Shame," he muttered and started walking.

Narrowing my eyes, I followed after him. Despite the strange urge I had to be near him, I imagined how it would feel to wrap my hands around his neck and cut off his air supply. I'd probably have to use the crook of my arm.

"You know, the least you could do is tell me how many days I've been here. How do you know when it's night?"

He strode a few more steps, then paused briefly. "Four."

My brows slammed down. "Four?"

"This is your fourth night here. Monsters are awake during the night and sleep during the day, so we count the nights."

Of course they do. I thought about the previous three ordeals I'd been through. "Each time, a different one of you has come to collect me. Shouldn't it have been the monster with the pointed ears' turn to get me?"

"Pointed ears? Oh, Kade. I'm taking you to him," he said over his shoulder.

I remembered what A-Two had said back in the room. *Kade doesn't like to wait. So the fourth monster is Kade.* I knew three of their names now, and for some reason, the thought made me feel a little powerful. Like the more I knew about these males, the more chance I had to survive them.

But I still wasn't looking forward to whatever this *Kade* had in store for me. "Any chance I can sit this one out?"

A-Two chuckled. "We've been looking forward to this all night."

Looking forward to it? Sadistic assholes. "So that's a no, then?"

He just chuckled again, his tail flicking from side to side as if it was mocking me. I had the sudden irrational urge to grab it to stop it from swishing around. My hand shot out, my fingers curling around the smooth length close to the pointed tip.

In a flurry of movement, A-Two whirled and threw my back against the rocky wall of the tunnel. My breath rushed out of me, and I stared in a daze, the soft tail still tight in my grip.

A-Two's hard face dropped close to mine, his eyes ablaze with fury. "What are you doing?" His voice was so cold, so full of anger, so unlike the way he'd spoken to me before that fear gripped my heart. His gaze slid to his tail in my grasp and then back to me.

I swallowed thickly, careful not to make any sudden movements. What the hell *was* I doing?

When I didn't respond, he dipped his face even closer to mine, his breath puffing on my cheeks. "Let. Me. Go." His command was clear, and I knew if I didn't do as he asked, things were about to go very badly for me.

Opening my fist, I released him, letting his tail fall from my fingers. His body shuddered as his tail was freed from my grasp, as though it had taken all of his control not to tear me to shreds. "Don't *ever* do that again," he rasped.

My heart beat painfully in my chest, but I set my jaw. "Fine."

Heaving out a breath, he lingered before me. Now that his tail was out of my hand, his entire demeanor changed, his whole body relaxing. My fingers itched, and I wasn't sure if I was wishing I was holding my dagger or trailing my fingers down the broad chest before me.

My dagger. The dagger this asshole took from me. Because he's a monster. You hate him, remember? I said the words in my mind, but I wasn't sure if I believed them. I should have been scared of him, and I was, but in that moment when I'd held his tail, it hadn't just been fury I'd seen in his eyes but...*pain.* Raw and blinding. And now I was wondering what could cause such pain.

You don't care, Raine. He tried to crush *you.* The reminder was enough to bring me to my senses. I shoved lightly against his chest, hoping it wouldn't be the final straw that shattered his control. "Get off me," I said, frustrated at how breathy my voice was.

Reluctantly, A-Two stepped away, his nostrils flaring. He gestured with his head toward the tunnel. "You first."

Clearly, he didn't trust me to walk behind him anymore. Normally, I would have thought of it as a small victory, but I couldn't stop seeing the fury and hurt in his eyes. I grasped the front of my dress to stop my fingers from shaking.

I understood then that aside from when I'd been almost crushed, this was the only other time I'd truly believed one of the monsters might kill me. Even when I'd stabbed A-Two in the shoulder, he'd had a lopsided smile on his face. *All righty then, don't touch a monster's tail.*

When my fingers stopped shaking, I forced my hips to sway with confidence, determined not to let him know how much he'd rattled me.

"Fucking trouble," I heard him mutter under his breath behind me, but I pretended not to hear him. I sauntered down the tunnel and acted as if I knew where we were going. I figured he'd tell me when I needed to take a turn, and I was right.

Eventually he started grunting out directions, leading us through the maze of tunnels. We were heading in a different direction than the other times I'd been led outside of my room, and I had the distinct feeling we were heading upward rather than down. It felt like an age later when we finally stopped before two huge iron doors.

Turning to A-Two, I tried to forget about the dread that was building inside me. "Any chance I can have my dagger back?"

He smirked at me. "As tempting as that is, I don't trust you with it."

"Me?" I asked incredulously, my brows lifting.

Ignoring my comment, he gestured with his head toward the doors. "Don't disappoint us, Sharachi."

I opened my mouth to make a retort, but he added, "Good luck."

I closed my mouth, momentarily stunned by the sincerity in his voice. With a nod, I stepped forward and pushed open the doors.

CHAPTER 13

~ **Raine** ~

Moonlight washed over my skin as I entered a large cavern, and I gasped, craning my neck upward to see the cavern was open above me. The pale moon was high and round, and stars spread across the sky, so beautiful and bright against the black.

Taking a deep breath, I inhaled the faint scent of crisp air. I'd been starting to wonder if I'd ever see the sky again. I had thought we were deep underground somewhere, but that wasn't it at all. *It's a mountain.*

Looking away from the stars, I forced myself to glance around at my surroundings. I didn't have time to think about where I was or how desperately I wanted to be outside. If the monsters had shown me anything, it was that they were consistent. Every time they led me somewhere, there had been something unpleasant waiting for me, and I assumed this time wouldn't be any different.

This cavern was a similar size to the last one I'd been in, but it had no water. Boulders of all shapes and sizes were spread out across the ground, many of the huge stones much taller and wider than I was.

A strange sliding sound came from behind me, and I turned to see the door vanish, replaced with a wall of rock. I wasn't going back out that way. *All right, you've been dropped down a pit, almost drowned, survived being in a room that tried to crush you, and were hypnotized by a water monster. It can't get much worse, right?* I didn't let myself answer. I had no doubt it *could* get a lot worse. In fact, my tortures so far hadn't been that bad, except when I'd been nearly crushed.

As if on cue, a low howl pierced the air, and the hairs on my arms stood on end. I darted behind the closest boulder and pressed myself against the cool stone, my pulse quickening as adrenaline spiked through my body. *Of course I'm stuck in here with some feral beast. Why not?*

I scowled as I thought of the horned monster who'd led me in there. *Really could have used my dagger right now, asshole.* Frowning, I scanned the area around me for any sharp object I could turn into a weapon, but there was nothing besides dirt, stones, and boulders. *Fuck.*

Another howl echoed through the cavern, and a chill pricked down my spine. *Not to worry, it's just a dog. A friendly dog. Not at all some horrible monster who wants to tear me to shreds.*

Swallowing, I cautiously poked my head out from behind the boulder, my gaze swiping across the area as I waited for a monster to materialize from the shadows. When moments passed and I spotted nothing unusual, I turned my attention to scoping out a possible desperate escape route.

I almost couldn't believe it when I saw a small cave opening high up along the back wall of the cavern. I blinked, wondering if my eyes were making me see things, but the cave remained.

The entrance to the cave was at least ten yards up the wall, but a mess of boulders lay beneath, and the wall itself was jagged and littered with rocky holds. *If I can climb to it, I might be able to escape the monster and this place. Or at least lose my captors enough to go searching for Cara.* I couldn't be sure what was up there. It could have been a dead end for all I knew, but it was *something*. Better than waiting around to become a monster's chew toy anyway.

Determination grounded me, and I clenched my jaw. I could do this. *Goddess, please let there still be nothing there.*

Holding my breath, I peered around the edge of the boulder again. When still nothing materialized from the shadows, I released the breath I was holding. I knew the monster was likely waiting for me to make a move, for me to step out into the open and become an easy target, but I couldn't stay hidden forever.

Keeping low to the ground, I dashed to the next closest boulder, heading toward the back of the cavern in the direction of the cave. This boulder was smaller than the last one, and I ducked my head to keep hidden. Every nerve in my body went on high alert as I prepared myself to run.

Now that I'd moved, I expected the monster to pounce, but the cavern remained eerily quiet, the sound of my breathing uncomfortably loud in the silence. I waited a moment longer before eyeing the distance to the next boulder. *Six yards to the right. That's not so bad.*

Shooting forward, I moved from boulder to boulder, nimble on my feet, my dress bouncing against my knees. I'd made it two-thirds of the way across the cavern without seeing whatever monster was in there with me, and hope began to bloom in my chest. *If I can just get to that cave, I can make it.*

I peeked my head around the side of the boulder I hid behind and my heart stuttered, my body stiffening. Almond-shaped golden eyes watched me from the other side of the cavern, glowing brightly in the darkness, and my heart began hammering as fear gripped me, choking me.

My throat dried out as I stared at the massive brown wolf standing on powerful legs. Its body reached as high as the huge boulder beside it, and every defined muscle was coiled as if the animal would spring forward at any movement.

The wolf lowered its head, its yellow gaze never leaving me, and the low growl that slipped between its peeled lips made the very stones at my feet shake.

Holy goddess. I didn't dare move. My chest rose and fell rapidly as I risked a glance at the small cave up the cavern wall. *If I can—* The wolf growled again, and I shuddered, quickly turning my attention back to the beast.

Did A-Two send me in here as dinner? And then I remembered. *Kade.* He'd said I was meeting Kade in there. The fourth monster. *But that would mean...* My thought trailed off as I stared disbelievingly at the wolf. Could the wolf *be* Kade? I wouldn't have believed it, but Darian's legs had transformed into a fishtail, so why couldn't A-Four turn into a wolf?

Whether the wolf was Kade or not, the beast didn't look happy. Its pointed ears twitched, and my panicked brain raced to think of a plan that didn't end in me dying. I was still too far from the cave. I was a fast runner, but I wasn't faster than a wolf. Especially one that size.

Cursing under my breath, I eyed the cave again and the path between the remaining boulders that I needed to take to get there. That cave was my only hope. I had to try. Blowing out a shaky breath, I gritted my teeth and ran.

· · · · ● · ● · · ·

~ Kade ~

The moment the human entered the cavern, my wolf detected her unusual scent. Traces of coconut and steel teased his nostrils, an intoxicating odor that made him salivate. The scent was like a breath of fresh air in comparison to the weak scent of berries and foliage that the other human had.

No, dominance leaked from this human, piquing my wolf's curiosity, and his senses heightened with excitement at the thought of a female who was strong enough to match him.

But my wolf didn't spring forward the moment he spied the human with the red hair. No, he remained still, waiting and watching as she made her way across the cavern, darting from boulder to boulder, his anticipation growing with every step she took.

She was smart, this one, only revealing herself in the brief time it took her to dash to another boulder, and constantly pausing as if waiting to see if he would emerge. Unfortunately for her, this just wound my wolf up more until curiosity drew him from the shadows.

When he stepped forward into the watery light of the moon, the human's amber gaze fixed on him from across the cavern, and the faintest scent of her fear had a rumbling growl escaping his throat. His body tensed, sharp black claws digging into the dirt. The humans always ran, and my wolf loved the chase.

But then she surprised him by sprinting further into the cavern in the direction of the back wall. The other human had turned and fled backward presumably to where she remembered the door being. But not this human. No, determination burned in her eyes as she sprinted closer to my wolf, passing him as his confusion bought her seconds.

But that's all it was. Seconds, and then he launched after her, his powerful body and huge paws quickly eating up the distance. He reached her just as she started scaling the fallen boulders resting at the back of the cavern, her fingers frantically grabbing onto the stone.

As soon as she started her ascent, I knew what she was doing. My wolf peered upward to where a small cave was carved from the rock, further up the wall. My brothers were about to get a visitor.

A frustrated growl tore from my wolf's throat, shattering the air, but the human continued climbing despite the rapid thudding of her heart. Her fingers clung to the rocks, bare toes gripping the stone as she moved out of reach.

Why hasn't she changed? This wasn't how it was supposed to go. Fear was supposed to bring on the change. All the other humans had already transformed, but not her.

My wolf jumped up, and his strong jaws snapped at her heels. His teeth missed by a mere inch, but she'd scaled the wall high enough that he couldn't get her. Not that it mattered. *Remember, we only want to terrify the human*, I reminded my wolf.

My wolf jumped up again, and his mouth opened wide just as she...slipped.

His huge jaws snapped shut, his long fangs sinking into warm flesh as the human's leg fell into his mouth. Lightning zapped through us as her skin touched my wolf's tongue, and pain seared down my wolf's throat, making him cough and splutter.

He hadn't been expecting to capture anything but air, and he gagged as blood filled his mouth, his sharp fangs buried deep into her flesh. Her weight knocked him backward, and he released her leg on instinct as both he and the human sprawled to the ground.

The lightning pain disappeared as soon as her skin disconnected with my wolf's tongue, and he jumped back to his feet.

The human remained on her back on the ground, red blood oozing from her leg, soaking her tattered white dress. She stared up at my wolf with wide eyes, all trace of fear replaced with...disappointment?

I took control, forcing my wolf back beneath my skin, my limbs shifting and morphing back to my human form. When the shift was complete, I crouched beside her, inspecting the wound on her thigh. It was fucking bad. Her blood gushed freely, red pooling onto the rocky ground, and I grimaced at the sight of what my wolf had done to her. There was too much blood.

My gaze lifted to her face, only to find she was looking at...a different part of me.

Heat rose in me as she continued to stare.

She blinked slowly, her gaze sliding up my chest, burning its way back to my face. Nudity wasn't something that bothered wolves, but I couldn't deny the effect her gaze had on me.

"Well, good for you," she said, her words slurred, and then her eyes closed.

· · · · ●· ●· · ·

The human was light in my arms as I carried her through the tunnels of the mountain, her head lolling to the side. *Raine*. That was what Darian had said her name was.

"What the fuck happened?" Locke asked as he, Asher, and Darian appeared behind me.

"He tried to eat her," Darian drawled, though he was striding quickly to keep up with us.

Asher peered at Raine's limp body. "Human's lost a lot of blood, Kade," he commented grimly. "You were only supposed to frighten her."

"I fucking know," I grumbled. "She fell."

Asher rubbed at his chest with his palm. "Fucking Halced, this pain."

Pain? I halted abruptly, and the others almost slammed into me. "What pain?" I growled, spinning toward him with my brows lowered.

Asher rubbed his chest again. "She's zapping me with something. My damn chest feels like it's on fire. It's been happening since she touched me."

"You feel it too?" Locke said in surprise, his dark eyes widening.

I glowered at the pair of them, unable to believe what I was hearing. "Why didn't you fucking say anything?" I thought of the searing pain in my chest that was growing in intensity, like something was trying to burrow to my heart.

"I thought it was just me," Locke said thoughtfully. "I didn't want to burden any of you until I knew what I was dealing with."

"We," Darian added, and the three of us turned to look at him.

He shrugged as if the fact he'd also been feeling the pain was no big deal. "I felt something when she grabbed my hand for the first time. I thought it was something to do with my own magic. Didn't feel anything the next time I touched her."

"Do you feel it now?" I barked. "The pain in your chest," I clarified. Fuck, my brothers were fools. We weren't supposed to keep secrets from one another.

Darian grimaced. "Unfortunately, yes. It's like something is trying to claw its way past my ribs. It's rather bothersome."

I grunted and continued striding down the tunnel with more haste than before.

"What's it mean?" Asher asked from behind me, staring over my shoulder at the red-haired human again.

"Since I touched her, I can feel her," I stated without looking back.

"She's in your arms, brother. Of course you can feel her," Asher said, a smirk in his voice.

"Not physically. It's like my wolf can feel her life force."

"I feel it too," said Locke, his face devoid of humor. "I just didn't fucking realize what I was feeling."

"And here I thought the human was just workin' her magic on me," Asher said.

"Whatever this feeling is, I'm guessing the fact her energy appears to be growing weaker right now isn't a good sign," Darian pointed out.

"No, it fucking isn't," I growled and started sprinting down the tunnel. I hated this. It wasn't just the pain. For countless years, I'd managed to keep a part of myself locked away. Buried deep so the memories didn't drive me mad. But as soon as the human had touched me, something inside me had changed.

It wasn't just that I could feel her life force, but it was the sudden urge I had to...*protect her*. The feeling had bile rushing up my throat, sweat streaming down the side of my face, and fear darkening my thoughts. Because I couldn't protect her. I couldn't protect anyone.

When I reached the door to our room, I didn't wait for Locke to open it. I kicked it open, tearing it off its hinges, and strode inside.

CHAPTER 14

~ **Raine** ~

A sharp pain lanced up my leg, bringing me back to consciousness, and I opened my eyes. It took a few blinks before I understood what I was seeing. Kade and A-Two crouched over me, way too close for my liking, and Locke and Darian stood watching close by.

I was surrounded by monsters. All four of them. *Fuck.* An increase in pressure on my leg sent a new wave of pain up my body, and I bit the inside of my cheek to stop from crying out. *Don't you dare, Raine. Don't give them that satisfaction. Just breathe.*

I forced myself to let out a shaky breath, and my gaze narrowed on where A-Two's large fingers probed around the brutal-looking bite mark on my thigh. His hand dangerously close to...

"He tried to EAT MY VAGINA!" The words were a strangled, surprised accusation.

Choked laughter and a snort sounded from Locke and Darian, and A-Two's hand stilled as he stared dumbly at me, but I wasn't looking at him. My gaze had pinpointed the monster who'd tried to kill me in the latest attempt. The wolf monster who'd sunk his fangs into my thigh.

No emotion showed on Kade's handsome face aside from the slight downturn of his brow, his golden gaze calm and assessing. He was still naked, the bulging muscles of his abdomen crunched as he squatted beside A-Two. I forced myself not to let my gaze fall lower than his belly, knowing full well if I did, I'd get another glimpse of his huge...

"You fell into my mouth," he said matter-of-factly, his voice a deep, rasping growl. "You shouldn't have run."

I pursed my lips. *Right. Don't run from the massive, angry wolf.* No wonder he had a massive cock. He *was* a huge dick. "You shouldn't have chased me," I retorted.

A-Two's fingers prodded at my wound again, sending an even worse stab of pain up my leg, and I almost lifted my good leg to try to kick him in the face. "A-Two, would you keep your damn hands to yourself!" I blurted.

A-Two's brow creased with confusion. "A-Two?" The horned monster didn't pull his fingers from my leg.

"Yeah, A-Two, as in, Asshole Two," I clarified, quite happy to call him an asshole to his face, seeing as the fucker had his fingers basically prodding my vagina, and not in a good way. "I know their names are Locke, Darian, and

Kade," I said, gesturing with my head to the others, "but I don't know yours. Asshole Two seemed fitting."

"Asshole Two," Darian mused thoughtfully, reaching a hand up to stroke his chin. "Well, that's downright delightful. I'm using that from now on."

A-Two glowered at the silver-haired male, but amusement shone in his eyes.

I licked my dry lips, suddenly more aware of my position. I was surrounded by monsters, wounded and vulnerable. And here I was, insulting them. Again. What was I thinking? "Uh, so I'll just be going back to my room now," I said. As much as I'd come to hate my little prison of a room, it was better than being here, surrounded by *them*. I leaned forward, and my face scrunched with pain at the movement. I blinked furiously, refusing to let the tears welling in my eyes spill down my cheeks. *Note to self: wolf bites hurt like a bitch.* A firm hand with violet nails pressed against my chest, forcing me back down on the cushioned chair, and I glared at A-Two.

"Tell you what. If I let you know my name, will you stop strugglin' so we can fix you up?" he asked.

"Fix me up?" I figured they weren't going to kill me, or they would have done it already, but I hadn't expected that they'd want to tend to my wound. My mouth popped open in surprise.

"You've lost a lot of blood," Locke said, his eyes dark. "If we don't do something, you'll die. You want us to save you, or you wouldn't have linked to us, right, *beautiful*?"

Linked to them? I didn't have the energy to question what he was talking about. My eyelids drooped, and I struggled to keep them open.

"Stay awake," Kade growled.

Pressure on my wound sent a new surge of pain through me, and my eyes opened wider.

"What did you do to us?" Kade asked, his voice cold.

I sucked a breath through my teeth at the pain, but a whimper slipped from my lips.

"She'll bleed out at this rate. Dar, the bottle," Locke snapped.

I watched as Darian grabbed a bottle of glowing blue liquid from an open medical kit spread near him and handed it to Kade.

I swallowed, still not quite believing that the monsters were trying to help me. *What if this is another torture they have planned? Why else would they pretend to help me?*

"Name's Asher," A-Two said, his violet gaze holding mine.

I stilled as I stared at him, my panic subsiding. There was something about those eyes that made me want to trust him, even though it went against everything I thought I knew. "Fine," I whispered.

Asher's answering smile left my stomach doing flips. "Good girl, Sharachi."

Sharachi? I was about to ask about the name he kept calling me when Kade's words cut my thought off.

"This'll hurt," the wolf monster interrupted and began pouring the blue liquid on the bite wound.

I tipped my head back and squeezed my eyes shut as the pain intensified, and an alcoholic smell filled my nostrils. *Fuck.*

"Why are you doing this?" I asked through gritted teeth, but I never heard the response as darkness crept over my vision and swallowed me whole.

• • • • • • • • • •

Opening my eyes, I found I was no longer in the same room as before but on a massive bed with pillows so soft they cradled my cheeks. The masculine scents of sandalwood and coffee surrounded me, and I wondered whose room I was in.

The pain in my thigh had dulled to an ache, and I frowned as I remembered Kade pouring the blue liquid onto my wound. *How long was I out?* The bite had been nasty, and it wouldn't have healed quickly.

Locke. Asher. Darian. Kade. I thought of the four monsters who had taken me from my island. I knew all their names now. Sure, they weren't as fitting as what I'd been calling them, but...*shit*. Knowing their names made them seem like more than just the monsters I'd grown up hating. I squashed the thought. They stole people from my island. They'd stolen Cara all those years ago, and they'd probably only saved me because they didn't want to lose their latest toy.

Peering around the dark room, I could only just make out a writing desk against one wall near a richly carved wardrobe. To my left, the door was cracked, letting a sliver of light spill onto the carpeted floor. Hushed voices sounded through the open door, and I strained my ears to make out the conversation.

"Raine's energy is returning. She'll be fine," said a lilting voice.

"Even if Kade's wolf tried to eat her," said a deep voice, a smirk in his tone. "What was that about bein' able to keep it in your pants, brother? As I recall, you weren't wearin' any."

"My wolf didn't eat her, for fuck's sake. She fell."

"Right, I'll use that excuse after my next hookup. The female will just 'happen' to fall onto my cock then too."

There was some grunting and the sound of shoving before someone grumbled. "At least that damn pain from my chest is gone."

A pause, and then a sharp voice. "It would have been better for her if she'd died. No one has gone through the fourth trial without changing. We all know what this means."

My brows lowered. *The fourth trial?* I remembered the wolf monster chasing me around the boulders in the cavern. It was the fourth ordeal they'd put me through. *It was a test?*

"We couldn't let her die. When her life force was weakening, ours was too. We all felt it. Until we sever whatever bond she's forged with us, we need to keep her alive. Besides, the Taratun council won't be happy if we lose a human."

Bond? These monsters are making no sense.

"Could she be a fae spy?"

A low growl. "It would explain the combat training she's had."

"She's too oblivious. Her methods too sloppy. She's had some training, but it's not at all like the fae Haraks art of fighting. More likely, she's a human trying to be a hero."

I scoffed. I wasn't trying to be a hero. I just wanted to save my sister. And what the hell were fae?

"Humans don't have magic," another voice pointed out. "And they certainly can't turn stone to sand or bond themselves to monsters. The magic of this mountain is changing her into something. We can't deny that."

"Her shock seemed genuine when she turned that rock ceilin' to sand. She might not even know she's bonded with us."

"Either way, we need to check in with the Taratun council soon, or they'll come looking for her," said a hard voice. "Warrick—"

"Who the hell are the Taratun?" I hadn't realized I'd voiced my question out loud until four monsters burst into the room, their hulking bodies looming over the end of the bed and their presence sucking the air out of the room. *Well, shit.*

"On," Kade barked, and blue torches high up on the walls flared to life, the glowing light making me wince.

Four gazes bored into mine—black, violet, blue, and gold, their monstrous figures at the end of the bed reminding me of a nightmare I'd once had years ago, shadows of horns, claws, wings, and pointed tails stretching on the wall. Though now, staring at these four, I wasn't sure if it would be a nightmare or some strange erotic dream. *Seriously, Raine? They're M-O-N-S-T-E-R-S.*

But my body wasn't listening. The same pull I'd been feeling toward Locke, A-Two—I mean Asher—and Darian, I also now felt for Kade, and with all four of them here, the feeling was so strong it was a small miracle I wasn't already stalking around the side of the bed toward them. Swallowing hard, I clenched my thighs together under the covers.

Four gazes tracked the slight movement of the blanket, and I had to resist the urge to fan my face. *Fuck. Me.*

"You're awake," Kade said, and I stopped myself from making some snarky comment about the astute assessment.

"Who are the Taratun, and why will they be looking for me?" I said bluntly, desperate to distract them from the fact I was lying on a bed before them. I didn't see any point in pretending I hadn't been listening to their conversation. I sat up, and the soft blanket covering me fell to my waist. Instead of my tattered white dress, a fine gray shirt hung loosely to my frame, the material sliding over my skin. "What the hell?" It was more of a question than a curse.

The monsters shared glances with one another, and it was Locke who spoke up, his onyx-colored eyes fixed on me, and his lips twisted into a dark smirk. "Kade didn't want your...dress ruining his bed. Not with all the blood and..." He trailed off with a wrinkle of his nose, and my cheeks flushed.

I knew my dress had smelled terrible. I'd been wearing the same garment for last few nights, and even with the dunking I'd received with Darian in the water, the dress was disgusting. But I wouldn't be embarrassed about that. It was their damn fault. No, what bothered me was the idea of all four of them stripping me bare while I was unconscious. I wasn't shy about them seeing me naked. It was only a body, after all. But the thought of being so vulnerable...

The monsters must have seen the fury building in my gaze as Asher added, "We only changed the dress and cleaned your wound. We didn't touch anythin' else."

Touch anything else. The words lingered, leaving a sour taste on my tongue, but a confusing heat flared low in my belly. The strange desire I had for them grew as I became even more aware of the fact that I was lying half-naked on a bed before four powerful, ridiculously attractive monsters. I narrowed my eyes. I couldn't be sure Asher was telling the truth, but would it change anything? I was still their prisoner.

"If you wanted me dead, you wouldn't have done...this," I said, gesturing to my body and the massive bed I was in. "If you're not going to kill me, the least you can do is give me some answers." I didn't expect them to tell me anything useful, but I had to try. "What do you mean I should have changed by now? Why am I here?"

For a moment, the four males were silent. Hidden messages were shared among their gazes, but then it was Kade who spoke, his voice a low rumble. "No one has gone through the fourth trial without turning. As of now, we're in uncharted territory."

My brows slammed down as annoyance tickled my temple. "What does that even mean? I should have turned into *what*?"

Locke smiled, but it wasn't a nice smile. The tips of pointed fangs protruded from his cruel lips. "A monster," he said, and the sharpness in his voice made me shiver.

"You still don't have the blood of a monster, beautiful," he continued. "The curse that plagues us should have turned you by now, but here you sit, the blood pumping through your veins still a crimson red. You're an anomaly in a world ruled by the creatures of the dark."

"Well, for now, at least," Kade added.

My brow creased. "The stone turning to sand. But that can't have been—"

"You," Asher finished for me. "You're turnin' into something. We're just not sure what yet."

Me? I thought of the strange energy I'd felt before the rocky slab had turned to sand. I assumed the monsters had just been toying with me, but to hear that it had been me was insane. These monsters were clearly crazier than I thought.

Locke's dark eyes were serious, pulling my attention back to him. "Thing is, beautiful, people will have questions. If you don't change soon, this could mean one of two things: either the curse has changed or you're turning into a monster we haven't seen since the curse was created. Either way, the Taratun council will take you and will likely run tests on you until they've satisfied their curiosity. Who knows what would be left of you then? Trust me when I say that however bad you think it's been the last few nights, it's nothing in comparison to how the Taratun would treat you."

I stared, a chill creeping down my spine as I processed his words. This wasn't good. Having the curiosity of these four was bad enough. I didn't want this Taratun to come looking for me. I had to escape before that happened. Despite the bleak news, there was something curious in what they were saying.

"The ones who turn into monsters," I blurted. "What happens to them?" I didn't care about me. Getting selected had only ever been about finding Cara, and if what they were saying was true, it meant they did have a purpose for the humans they took from my island. *My sister might be alive.* Sure, she might have also been a monster, but I wasn't going to worry about that then.

"Are you even listening, Raine lovely?" Darian said, exasperated. "You haven't turned into a monster. Not fully. That's the problem."

I ignored him. "Do you kill them?" I asked, training my intense gaze on Kade. After the almost-biting-my-vag thing, I felt like he was the one who owed me answers the most.

He held my stare, his golden eyes not leaving mine. "The fate of the newbloods is not our concern right now. What is of concern is how you bonded us." His face hardened.

My jaw clenched, and I found my fingers automatically searching in the sheets, hoping for some phantom weapon.

A monster would sleep with a dagger under his pillow, right? No, just me, then? "How I what?" I said, my heartbeat quickening.

"You should just answer him, lovely," Darian said, unamused. "He won't let this go."

I glared, my muscles twitching with anticipation at the crackle of energy in the air. "I don't know what you're talking about."

Kade stared at me for a painfully long time, but Asher let out a chuckle, breaking the silence. "Well, this is going to be fun."

Locke turned to the others. "Kade, tell Lyr we're going to need to call in that favor she owes us. Ash and Dar, visit the newbloods. Find out if any of them are exhibiting unusual abilities. And keep an ear out in case anyone's making noise about the missing human. I'll take the first watch with our...guest." He fixed a predatory gaze on me, and I grabbed the edge of my shirt under the blanket, crunching the fabric in my fist.

Without another word, the monsters filed out of the room.

CHAPTER 15

~ Asher ~

"Hmm yes, Asshole Two suits you perfectly," Darian said with a teasing smirk, pretending to analyze me as we strode down the tunnel.

"Fuck off," I said with a laugh, shoving him hard enough that he stumbled on his next step before gracefully correcting himself.

Flicking an invisible speck of dirt off his shirt, he smoothed his hands down his chest as he walked. "Maybe if you had treated our lovely Raine nicer from the beginning, she would have given you a better nickname."

I gave Darian an incredulous look. "We are supposed to terrify the humans to get them to turn faster. It's our job."

"That's no excuse for poor manners."

"As I remember, you almost had her jumpin' you when you were in the water. Did you ask her politely before makin' her straddle you?" I said with a grin.

A wicked smile lifted his lips. "I wasn't going to let it go far. How was I to know she'd bonded us? I just needed to know what would happen if she touched me again. The female is very interesting..."

"You're tellin' me. Whatever this link is that she's created, just bein' around her makes my dick hard. It's bloody torture."

"You and me both," he said with a chuckle.

We walked in silence for a short while, our footsteps echoing along the tunnel when he asked, "How do you think the newbloods are going?"

Sighing, I ran a hand through my hair. "I'm guessin' as well as can be expected."

"What do we have? A vamp, three demons, one ogre, one incubus, three sirens, a banshee, and a bear shifter. The Taratun will be happy."

I didn't answer, my attention on the huge iron doors up ahead, guarded by two minotaurs. Thick black horns reached out from the sides of the guards' bull-shaped heads, and wide golden bands wrapped around their muscled biceps, indicating their service to the Taratun council. We stopped before them, and the guards peered at us with small black eyes.

"Hi there, fellas, if you'll be so kind as to open the doors for us," I said with a smile. I wondered if that was polite enough for Darian.

The guard on the right tightened his grip on a double-headed battle-ax. "We don't follow the commands of deserters," he snarled.

Darian shifted beside me, and I knew he was readying himself for a fight. The pair of us could have crushed them if we wanted. The Taratun's guards were trained well, but against the two of us, they'd stand no chance. They knew it too, but they also wanted to have their say.

Monsters always stayed with those of their kind. Vampires stayed with vampires, demons stayed in houses that contained demons, and so on. The fact my brothers and I had made our own odd clan bothered a large portion of the monster community. We only got away with it because we were four of the strongest monsters to grow up in this hellhole. That, and thanks to Locke's father, but that sadistic asshole had his own agenda and made Locke pay for his help.

I knew the council would find a way to break us up eventually. But I'd do whatever I could to keep us together. Like hell was I going back to join the House of Thorem, the high house of demons. And if the price of us being together was dealing with this shitbag, then I was all right with that.

"Ah now, don't be like that. We're still around. You don't need to be salty about missin' us."

The guard's face scrunched with anger. "You four are not fit to be in this mountain. Go back to the slums where you've been hiding."

"Now that's enough," Darian drawled, but his gaze was sharp. "We all know you're letting us in there. We have official business with the Taratun, and if you don't let us in, we'll make you. Save yourself the bruises and open the doors."

"They're not worth it," the other guard muttered to his comrade, opening the door on his side.

The first guard spat on the ground with disgust, but he opened the other door. "Your time will come, deserters."

"Lookin' forward to it," I said with a wink and strolled through the door.

· · · · ● · ● · · · ·

We entered the common room of the newbloods, and I wrinkled my nose at the scent of blood. Iron doors lined the sides of the cavern, and I knew they led to the separate sleeping quarters and washrooms of the newly turned, and to individual training rooms so the monsters could learn to control their abilities.

A fire crackled in the fireplace at the back of the room, and the walls were lined with elaborate paintings of Katakin city, the pictures in gilded frames. For the next three nights, the newbloods wouldn't leave this area. Had the human, Raine, turned, she would have been there as well.

My brows lowered at the thought. The idea of the human leaving our rooms to stay here under the care of the Taratun didn't sit right with me.

Four monsters were seated at the large dining table in the middle of the room, a large jug of pink liquid among them, and the same liquid also in their cups. The newbloods turned to stare at us, and my chest lifted, my back straightening.

I remembered watching each of them turn. The vampire from the first trial, the pretty female with raven-black hair and plump red lips, sipped from a vial of blood, watching Darian and me with an interested gaze. Her tongue slipped over the tip of the glass vial, licking at the red liquid seductively as she eyed us greedily. *Well, fuck me.* She was going to fit right in, that one.

Beside her sat two females, both with pale-blonde hair that shimmered in the firelight. I knew they were sirens, having watched them change during Darian's trial, but if I hadn't, their glowing blue eyes and the scent of the sea on their skin would have given them away.

My attention went to the last newblood at the table, *a demon*. Small green horns protruded from her chestnut-colored hair, and a long green tail was suspended in the air behind her, flicking as she watched me with pale-green eyes, a small smile on her face. She had turned during the second trial, the moment I'd pulled the lever and the rocky ceiling had started descending toward her.

Sweat beaded on my brow, my skin becoming clammy as the image of another face appeared in my mind. Of a woman with sleek coffee-colored hair and eyes that shone like opals when she smiled. My mother's face.

I scratched at my arm without realizing as the image slipped away, changing into another, the one that showed the truth of what had happened. My mother's face appeared contorted, her eyes gleaming with madness.

This was the mother I'd last seen. A mother who had cut off her own tail after the curse had turned her into a demon. The one who, in her crazed mind, had thought mutilation was the way to make us human again. A stream of sweat slid down my neck as I tried not to think about it, but the memory broke through.

I pictured my mother's face as she'd stepped toward me when I was only five years old, a child and a newblood. She'd held a kitchen knife in her hand, the cruel blade still dripping with her own black blood. *"It will only hurt for a moment, darling, and then we'll remove our horns. You'll see. We'll be human again,"* she'd said, her mad eyes wide and unnatural on her sweet face.

I'd just watched her, unable to move. Fear and confusion rooting me to the spot. None of the other monsters had intervened, not even when I'd cried out for help. It had been months since the curse was created, and we'd only just moved to the House of Thorem, the huge estate that housed the high-level demons of the city.

But the other demons didn't care about a young boy, and my father, who'd turned into a wraith, had left us to live in the House of Faren, the high house of shadows.

My mother had almost grabbed me when I'd scrambled to the window and just jumped, without thinking, from the third floor. I'd landed wrong, breaking my leg, but my body had healed quickly, and I'd escaped from that house. Escaped *her*. The mother I'd loved with my whole heart.

It was Locke who'd found me sobbing on the cobblestones a couple blocks away. He was only two years older than me at the time and still getting used to his own vampire body, but he'd helped me when no one else had.

I remembered the human, Raine, grabbing my tail in the tunnel. Even now, I couldn't stand anyone touching it. *Fucking hell.* I'd nearly killed Raine for that. I'd been so close, and it had only been her coconut-and-steel scent, so incredibly different from the scents of rose and flour that my mother had, that had helped me to see clearly. To control myself.

I played my fucking part in these trials because that was what we had to do. To appease Locke's father. To make sure the four of us could stay together without the council ripping us apart, forcing us back into the houses they thought we belonged to. I wasn't going back to the House of Thorem. Not ever. And if that meant I had to be a part of the trials, I'd keep my shit together. I'd pretend it was all a game, and if any of the newbloods showed any signs of madness, I'd be the first to volunteer to end their lives.

"You all right?" Darian's voice floated to me, his long fingers curling over my shoulder.

I jerked, instinctively trying to pull away, but he held on, holding me firm, grounding me.

I took a deep breath. And another. Then I turned to him, pushing any thought of my mother to the dark recesses of my mind, and plastered a wide smile on my face. "Sure am, brother."

He nodded, but I knew he didn't believe me.

"Ah, Darian, my favorite siren," a smooth feminine voice called out to us, and we turned as Perene strolled over, her perfect black-painted lips pulled into a smile. Her ebony gaze fixed on Darian, and I smirked at the way she blatantly admired his physique.

Stopping in front of us, she lifted her hand to Darian. He took her hand in his, pressed his lips to her pale flesh, and pulled back to give her a sensual smile. "My lady Perene, it is a pleasure to see you as always."

Perene preened under his gaze, but her face soured when she turned her attention to me. As expected, she didn't offer me her hand. "Asher," she said with a nod, but I didn't miss her hint of distaste.

Even though I'd never shown any of the signs of madness like my mother had, some of the monsters kept their distance, as if the fools thought whatever had happened to her was contagious or was a disease that ran in my bloodline.

I just smiled widely, baring my teeth. "Perene," I said lightly.

She tilted her head then, her brow furrowing as she peered around us, though it was obvious we were alone. "Have you come to bring me the last newblood?"

"Not yet," Darian drawled, his voice silky smooth. "Locke wishes to have longer with the female. He's enjoying toying with the little shifter too much."

"Ah, so she turned into a shifter," Perene mused, not at all concerned by the idea that her son would enjoy torturing a newblood.

Darian's relaxed persona didn't waver. "Yes, the human turned during the fourth trial. It was all rather predictable."

I was glad Darian was the one talking. Locke had previously explained to us his plan to pretend Raine had turned into a shifter, but I had no doubt the vampire bitch would be able to sense my lies.

I loathed Perene, and lying convincingly wasn't part of my skill set. Darian, however, had grown up in the House of Saceris, the high house of water monsters. From what he'd told me, the monsters in that house were as vain as they came, with tongues as sharp as vipers'. No, this time, I was more than happy to let him take the lead.

"Such a shame," Perene said, her perfect lips forming a pout. "I was hoping for another vampire to add to the House of Nesarin. Not to worry. Miss Lana is proving to be quite the addition." She motioned with her head toward the vampire seated at the table. The dark-haired female was still watching us, but she'd discarded her now empty vial. A tight navy dress was fitted to her body, and she leaned forward, her elbows resting on the table and her breasts practically falling out of her dress.

"Oh, how so?" Darian asked, his gaze trailing from Lana back to Perene.

"She's taken to being a vampire splendidly. It's not easy taming bloodlust, you know, but she has been quite formidable. You should tell my son to stop playing with that...shifter," she said, her top lip curling, "and come visit me here."

My gaze went back to Lana, who smiled a saccharine smile that did nothing to hide the new darkness in her eyes. Gone was the human who had trembled when Locke had selected her back on the island, and in its place was a predator. A vampire. A monster.

I knew Locke would want nothing to do with her. He didn't hate vampires like I hated the demons, but he hated his father and all that the House of Nesarin stood for. He wasn't about to claim the new vampire and follow in his parents' footsteps.

"We'll be sure to tell him," Darian said, though he had to be thinking the same thing I was.

"So the newbloods are progressin' well?" I prodded, wanting to get out of there as quickly as possible.

Perene's sharp gaze cut to me. "They're all adjusting well enough." She paused, and her gaze became suspicious. "Why did my son really send you here? He knows the Taratun council has this in hand. *I* have this in hand."

"Warrick asked Locke to check in on your progress," Darian drawled. "Locke sent us in his stead."

The female vampire sighed, the suspicion leaving her eyes. "Between my husband who never leaves his lab and my son who avoids me at every opportunity, it's like I have no family at all. You can tell Locke all is well, and he'd better finish playing with the last newblood and bring her to me soon. There are only three nights before the Week of Orash begins, and the shifter will be expected to participate, as will all the newbloods. We can't have a monster without a house to belong to."

I ignored Perene's barb at us not belonging to one of the houses.

"Of course," Darian said with a smile. "We'll tell him."

CHAPTER 16

~ Raine ~

I sat in the darkness for a long while, the room feeling like an empty void now that the monsters weren't looming over the end of the bed.

It was all too much. This was supposed to be simple. Get chosen. Try not to die. Escape the monsters and find Cara. Fine, not simple, but simpler than whatever the hell this was. It was clear I was part of some sort of experiment. They expected me to turn into one of them, and the fact that I hadn't yet changed had complicated things. A dark laugh slipped from me, and I rubbed a hand down my face. *Fuck.*

And what were the monsters talking about when they mentioned a bond? They thought it was me who'd linked to them? They were obviously delusional. But even as I thought it, something inside me was urging me to get out of bed. To go find the monster who I knew was on the other side of the door. I groaned.

Collecting myself, I slid off the bed, planting my bare feet on the carpeted floor. The plush material was soft between my toes, nothing at all like the cold stone floor of the room I'd been in for the last few nights. Taking a step forward, I was surprised at the lack of pain in my thigh.

As I ran a hand up the bottom of the long shirt and along my thigh, my fingers passed over the bumps of the bandage wrapped around my leg. I'd seen what the bite had looked like. It was nasty and felt just as bad as it looked. *"We only changed the dress and cleaned the wound,"* Asher, the demon with the horns and tail, had said. How could my leg be this healed if they'd only cleaned it?

I padded to the door and entered the adjoining room. The space was large, with blue flames flickering in an ornate fireplace, plush settees, numerous tables, and an entire wall filled with weaponry. My gaze snagged on the expertly crafted swords, daggers, axes, spears, and an array of other weapons that I didn't even know the names of.

"Don't get any ideas," said a smooth masculine voice, and my gaze snapped back to the other side of the room. Locke lounged on a bloodred settee, an open book on his lap.

Monsters...read? Even more surprising was the monster's appearance. Where I'd always seen long black claws were soft, rounded fingertips, and instead of eyes that were an unnerving black, white surrounded the dark pupils, making the male seem almost...normal. Well, maybe not normal—he was still ridiculously handsome—but he almost looked *human*. *Where are his wings?*

As if he knew why I was gaping, his lips twisted as he gave me a dark smile. "Not what you expected?"

I cleared my throat. It didn't matter if he could control when to show his true monster side. I knew what he was.

"What did you do to me?" I asked, my hand reaching down again to my thigh, though the bandage was covered by the gray shirt that reached almost to my knees.

Locke's dark gaze trailed down my body, scanning from my face down to where the shirt ended just above my knees, and then back to my face again. I clenched my jaw, refusing to let my body tremble at the look he'd just given me.

"I think you mean 'thank you.' And you're welcome, beautiful."

I glared at his incessant use of the nickname *beautiful*. Coming from his mouth, it almost sounded like a plea. Or a curse. "How long was I out?" I asked, my voice hard.

He cocked his head as if he was thinking. "Six hours, give or take."

My eyes widened. "Six hours? But how?"

"Let's just say the water here isn't the same as what you're used to. If you were one of us, the wound would have healed much quicker. Some monsters heal instantly," he said.

Monsters like Asher. I hadn't forgotten how the horned demon's wound had healed almost immediately after I'd stabbed him. Were these four all like that?

Locke didn't appear to be moving from his relaxed position, so I decided to venture closer, all the while keeping the wall of weapons in my peripheral vision. I dropped onto the red settee closest to the fire, the one furthest away from the monster. My wound may have been much better, but it still ached, and the ache grew the longer I was standing. *Damn wolf.*

A moment passed with me eyeing Locke warily, and the heat of the fire warmed my cheeks, making me sweat beneath the shirt. Or was I just sweating because the onyx-eyed monster was still staring at me as if I was prey? "What are you going to do with me?" I finally asked.

He raised a brow. "Right now"—he motioned to the food on the table in front of me—"eat. Drink. We can't have you dying while we're bonded."

"I don't know anything about a bond," I said, ignoring the food. "And even if I could bond to others, I certainly wouldn't tie myself to you assholes."

His jaw twitched, but he simply gestured to the food again with his head. "Eat."

I stared at the silver platter piled with fruits, cheeses, and cuts of meat. Something in the monster's tone made me think that if I didn't eat soon, he'd force the food down my throat. A part of me wanted to refuse, just to defy him, but my stomach growled, empty and aching.

For days now, all I'd had was crusty bread, and I could hardly remember when the last time was. Before the last trial? If I didn't eat something soon, I wouldn't have the energy for any type of escape.

Cautiously, I picked a slice of some type of cured meat and placed it in my mouth. The tantalizing taste of salt and savory danced on my tongue, and I had to stop myself from letting out an embarrassing moan. But seriously, had anything ever tasted so good?

As if I'd unleashed something inside me, my fingers became swift, plucking grapes, cheeses, and other foods off the platter, savoring and relishing them. There was fruit that looked like stars, and cheeses with holes so big my fingers could slip through. I had the fleeting thought that maybe a rat had started eating the food on the platter, but at this point, I didn't really care. *Goddess, so good.*

"If you don't slow down, you'll be heaving all that up soon. I'm not cleaning the mess," said Locke, watching me with amusement.

Has he been staring at me the whole time? Of course he would have been. I stilled my gaze, then slid it to Locke, who sat watching me with interest, his own gaze razor-sharp. Had I really just forgotten he was there? I swallowed and chastised myself for letting my guard down.

He gestured with long pale fingers to the silver goblet on the table. "If you need to wash all that down."

I eyed the liquid. The silver goblet was deep, and the liquid was dark. *Wine?* "What is it?" I almost didn't care. I was just excited to see something to drink other than the sweet pink liquid they'd been feeding me.

"Something we all drink here, or we die."

Die? Well, that's a way to bring me back to reality. I frowned, unsure whether to drink it. A challenge shone in Locke's gaze. *Right. Dead if I don't drink this. Well, if we're bonded as they think, whatever the hell that means, then they don't want me dead. Here goes.* I lifted the silver cup to my lips.

The liquid was warm and thick and... "Ugh!" I spat the rest of my mouthful, liquid dripping down my chin and flying onto the small table before me, showering crimson over the remaining fruits, cheeses, and meat arranged on top of one another as if they were art.

Before I even had the chance to wipe my face, Locke was before me, tilting my head up to face him, his fingers gripping my chin painfully. I hadn't even seen him move. His black gaze peered into my own as if he was looking for something. Searching for secrets in my eyes.

I tried to wrench my chin from his grip, but his claws pricked against my flesh.

"What was that?" I rasped, a coppery taste still on my tongue.

"Blood."

Bile threatened to rush up my throat, and I swallowed to stop myself from gagging. "Why would you give me that? You said it was something you all drink or you die?"

"By 'we,' I meant those like me."

"Like you?"

"Vampires," he said as if he was surprised that I didn't already know the answer.

"Whose blood do you drink?" My face paled as I thought of the other villagers. As I thought of Cara.

His nose dipped down then, and his fangs brushed along my neck, his hot breath on my skin. He inhaled, and my stomach gave a strange flip. My body trembled, wanting to be near him. With him. The bond pulling us closer.

What the actual—? I didn't let myself think. My knee struck out, slamming into Locke's crotch. He doubled over in pain, and the distraction was enough. I wrenched my chin from his grip and launched toward the shelf of weapons.

If I can grab a weapon, I can—

Two yards from the shelf, my gaze set on a pair of knives, long clawed fingers wrapped around my shoulder and jerked me around. Stepping forward, Locke pushed me against the bare wall on the right, my back connecting with smooth stone. His wings were back again, flared above his shoulders, and his intense eyes were like black pools of night.

He leaned toward me and fisted the front of my shirt, making the gray material ride up my thighs. "Kick me there again, and you'll beg for me to hand you over to the Taratun." His voice was low, promising violence.

Glaring, I squirmed against him, but he held me fast. All my struggling was doing was making my shirt lift further up. "Let me go," I hissed.

His dark gaze dropped to my bare thighs and trailed upward until it lingered on my neck. As he continued to stare, his mouth parted slightly, showing his long white fangs. His breathing was heavy, his muscles twitching as if he was trying to stop himself from lashing out. *Fuck. Is he going to bite me?*

A confusing surge of excitement went through me. I should have been terrified. Here was death personified, and I wasn't sure if I wanted to headbutt him or let him draw me closer. A strange energy lured me toward him. I inhaled, taking in his intoxicating scent of cedarwood, ash, and spice. I hated him, but I *wanted* him. I wanted to feel the hard press of his body against mine, and his fingers sliding up my thighs.

"If you're going to kill me, just do it," I finally managed to say. I was sick of this. This stupid game they'd thrust me in. Their experiment, whatever the hell it was. So many questions and riddles it made my eyes hurt. They'd saved me but for what? To keep playing with me? I didn't want to die—I needed to find Cara—but something told me if I moved right then, I might have snapped whatever control this monster had.

His gaze slid to mine, and he leaned even closer. Close enough that his breath puffed on the side of my face. Finally releasing my shirt, he lifted an arm above me, placing his palm against the wall as if he was bracing himself against the stone. Slowly, his breathing began to calm. "What are you?" he said in a rasping whisper, and I wasn't sure if he was expecting me to answer.

I opened my mouth not sure what I would say, when the door to the room opened and Ash and Darian strolled inside, followed by Kade.

They stopped when they saw us, taking in how Locke had me pressed against the wall. Now that he'd released my shirt, the gray material reached back toward my knees, but that didn't stop the warmth from growing in my cheeks as I took in their amused gazes. The three other monsters turned from us and strolled right past, making themselves at home in the room.

"Lyr will be here within the hour," Kade growled as he dropped onto a settee.

As if pulled from a trance, Locke pulled his hand away from the wall and strode over to the others, leaving me glaring after him.

I remained where I was, watching as Asher picked at the platter of food, not at all bothered by the droplets of blood that had speckled over the display.

My gaze flitted to the shelf of weapons, and I sighed, turning back to the monsters. All four of them were sitting now, and Locke had his book propped back on his lap as if nothing had happened.

"I fed her blood," Locke said to the others, speaking as if I wasn't in the room.

"Looked like you were doin' more than that," Asher said with a grin, stuffing a rolled piece of cured meat into his mouth.

"What happened?" Kade asked, his face hard.

"Nothing," Locke said, and for a moment, I wasn't sure if he was talking about the blood or...something else. "Not even a glimmer of black in her gaze when she drank the stuff."

Right. The blood. You're officially an idiot, I scolded myself.

"I'm still here," I said, irritated that they were talking about me as if I was nothing but a fly on the wall. I moved closer to them, though I didn't know why I wanted to draw their attention back to me. Four gazes slid my way, and I stopped where I was halfway across the room, wishing I'd kept my mouth shut.

"Like we could forget, lovely," Darian said with a smile. *Goddess,* he was beautiful. The male had the face of an angel. *Tail. The monster has a freaking fishtail when he's in water,* I reminded myself. But it was hard to convince myself that was even true.

"If you're going to keep me caged here like some animal, the least you can do is tell me what you have planned for me," I said, determined not to lose my nerve. I was so damn tired of these assholes.

To my surprise, they didn't dismiss me.

Asher swallowed his latest mouthful and spoke. "There's no point keepin' her in the dark about everything. She's part of this world now. Better that she knows what's goin' on, so she's prepared if the Taratun take her."

Locke's jaw ticked, but he gestured to an unoccupied space on the settee near Asher. "Sit," he commanded.

"I'll stand, thanks," I said, glowering back at him.

"Suit yourself."

"You've told me that you expect me to turn into a monster. But why? What is all this?" I opened my arms, gesturing to the room when I really meant the past few nights. The offerings. Everything I knew about this place. I folded my arms in front of my chest.

"We don't have time for this," Kade growled.

"If we don't explain some of this, our sweet Raine is going to get herself killed trying to escape," Darian said, sipping from a goblet. "She doesn't understand the severity of her situation. And ours."

Kade grunted, and I wasn't sure if it was him voicing his agreement.

Locke lifted his chin. "Ash, will you do the honors?"

The horned male grinned and turned his attention to me. "Story time, Sharachi."

I forced myself not to roll my eyes, but really, I was nervous. What horrible things would they tell me about my fate? About Cara's fate?

"Starts over two hundred years ago, when our charmin' King Adrien married a fae princess," Asher began.

"Fae?" I moved a step closer.

"Magical bein's from another world," Asher explained as if knowing of other worlds was common knowledge. *Ass.* "The marriage was supposed to unite our kingdoms, but King Adrien was greedy. On a trip to the fae world, he killed their king, breakin' the treaty and dooming our people, effectively declaring war. The princess was heartbroken to hear of her father's murder, and she confronted King Adrien, her husband. It didn' go well, to say the least." He let out a dark chuckle.

"She cursed the king to become a monster, as that's what he called the fae people, monsters. He was bound to this land, unable to die, but unable to really live. Problem was, the curse didn' just affect the king. No, the queen's fae magic affected the whole city, turning everyone into all manner of monsters. No one with human blood was spared."

My jaw dropped. *These males, these monsters...they used to be human?*

"Every human that comes here turns within nights," Darian finished for him. "The curse has remained the same until now. Until you, that is."

I blinked slowly as I processed their words, feeling both small and too big for my skin at the same time. *Me?* I was a nobody. Just a girl from a village who was stupid enough to get her sister selected for the offering before her time. Who'd practiced fighting every day since in the hopes she could one day fight against the monsters.

"The higher a human's heart rate, the more in distress they are, the faster they change," Locke spoke, his voice cold. "So for the next few nights, we'll be testing you at every opportunity. Anything we can think of, we'll be throwing your way. And you'd better hope you change soon."

"But if I don't turn, doesn't that mean the curse is broken? Won't your people be...happy?"

Asher laughed. "Some may see it that way. Others..." he trailed off before continuing, "they like living in the darkness. The immortality. The strength. Either way, you'll become a target."

I nodded, though his words hadn't really sunk in yet. All I needed to know was, "What happens to the ones who turn? Where are the others from my village?" *Where is Cara?* I needed answers.

"Well, ya see," Asher began, but Locke cut him off.

"They become part of our society, our world," Locke said sharply.

Become part of their world? When Locke didn't elaborate, my brows slammed down. There were unspoken words in his gaze, and I would find out what the hell he was keeping from me, but for now, only one thought went through my mind. *That means Cara could be alive.*

The thought sent a surge of hope through me, and tears pricked my eyes. I'd suspected Cara might be alive, but it was only now that they'd admitted they didn't kill the newbloods. My sister hadn't been tortured to death. She was likely somewhere in this damned place, and I was going to find her. A little of the guilt that haunted me began to lift.

I forced myself to process the other bits of information the monsters had given away. "If the fact I'm still human could mean an end to the curse, shouldn't you want to turn me over to this Taratun council you keep speaking about?" From the sounds of it, I definitely did not want that to happen, but I needed to understand their motivations. Why were they keeping me here?

"You've bonded with us," Kade said.

"So you've said, but no one is explaining what that means."

"The first time you touched each of us, did you feel anything?" Darian asked, his eyes sparkling.

I remembered the searing pain that had spread throughout my whole body, and my eyes narrowed in accusation. "Yes, because you guys did something to me."

Asher shook his head. "Our powers aren't like that. Somehow, we're all bonded now, and when your energy weakened—"

"So did ours," Kade finished.

They didn't look at all happy about what they were telling me, but I couldn't find it in myself to feel bad. I hadn't done anything, so someone else had created this bond, and also, these assholes had just spent the last few nights torturing me and the other villagers. They deserved so much worse.

"So...you think if I die, you might die too?"

"Yes," Locke said.

I smiled, and before I could help it, laughter bubbled up out of my throat.

A menacing growl ripped through the air, and I stopped myself midlaugh, somehow managing to control myself. Kade's gaze was dangerous, as if he was about to attack me.

I licked my dry lips and didn't miss the fact his gaze tracked the movement. "So let me get this straight: you expected to torture me until I turned into a monster, but instead, we're now linked, and you can't kill me because that would also kill you too? You also can't hand me over to the Taratun, as they might kill me, which, again, would kill you?"

"We also have enemies who would love this information," Darian added as if he was as amused by the situation as I was. "We're immortal, but there are ways to kill us."

"Though, it's near impossible," Asher said with a smirk.

"Killing a human is much easier," Kade growled, and his eyes were haunted as he said it.

"So for now we have to keep you a secret," Locke said. "Whatever you're turning into, we need to get the change to happen faster and hope no one hears of this."

CHAPTER 17

~ Locke ~

The damn human would be the death of us. Her body was fragile, but she seemed to care nothing for it, doing whatever she could to infuriate me.

It had taken all my effort to keep from biting her. The urge to sink my fangs into her neck had been almost irresistible, the scent of her sweet blood pushing the limits of my control. And that was not all I wanted to do to her. I pictured Kade's gray shirt sliding up, revealing her bare thighs.

Fucking Halced. I'd never wanted anyone this badly before. I'd had my share of females, but I'd always been in control, and they'd never been anything more than a way to let out my frustrations for the night, just like I had been for them.

If Raine didn't turn soon, I couldn't be held responsible for what happened to her. Monsters and humans were not meant to coexist.

It didn't bother me that we'd told her of the past of the Katakin. The human was a part of our world now whether she wanted to be or not, so there was no point denying her the truth. At least, the part she needed to know.

When I'd scented her in that clearing on the island mere nights ago, I'd only selected her thinking she would be a hearty distraction. That body certainly was. But had something else compelled me to select her? I'd never believed in the gods. I had grown up in a world of monsters, and gods didn't live where the dark things roamed.

The magic that bonded us together now called to me. Even at this moment, it urged me to get closer to her. To be with her. To...protect her. It wasn't just that we would die when she died. The magic was compelling me to protect this human. I could feel it with every part of my dark being.

Whatever this was, someone wanted me to keep this human alive. Whether it had been created by Raine's own subconscious, a defense magic she'd unknowingly unleashed when she'd come here, perhaps a byproduct of whatever monster she was turning into, I couldn't be sure.

All I knew was that unfortunate things would happen to my brothers and me if anything bad was to befall her. A fate of hers that was becoming more likely with every night she remained alive. With every night she remained human.

Fuck. I couldn't let my father take her. The outliers were bad enough—the monsters without a conscience. They would be a danger to our kind anyway. But not this human. Her attitude was...refreshing. A wake-up call to my dark soul.

A knock sounded on the door to our common room, and my gaze tracked Darian as he glided to the door, his long limbs moving as gracefully as if he was in water.

Finally. I stood as the iron door opened.

"Lyr, it's wonderful to see you," Darian greeted the newcomer.

"Darian, as eloquent as ever," the lithe female said with a smirk, kissing Darian on the cheek and sauntering into the room. Small lilac flowers were twisted into the snow-white braid that trailed down her back, and I guessed one of her mates had put them there. The shifter wore her usual leathers and boots, the supple material molding sinfully to every curve of her body.

Behind her strode Dean, the mate who I suspected had used his magic to weave the flowers into her hair. The male's kind olive-green eyes crinkled as he smiled at Darian, and I noted the black leather case he held at his side. "Darian," Dean said with a nod.

Darian greeted the male and shut the door.

Lyr's gaze swept across the room, and she strutted forward toward Kade, who was the next closest. "Kade, I was surprised when Dean said you visited the house," she said and planted a kiss on his cheek. "You could have come inside."

Kade wrapped his arms around her, embracing her, and then set her back on her feet. "I was only there to deliver a message."

Dean tensed as he watched them from nearby, his muscles twitching beneath his green skin, but he said nothing. I used to think Lyr's mates were foolish. The way Dean, Nic, and Soren would always keep close to Lyr's side, ready to protect her against any foe, had always seemed...unnecessary. Especially when Lyr was one of the strongest females I knew, and certainly did not need protecting. But now, when I thought of someone going near Raine who was keeping out of sight in Kade's room, I felt the instinct rise in me. I clenched my jaw, bringing my attention back to the situation at hand.

When she finished greeting the others, Lyr spun toward me. "Locke," she said, her lips upturned. "You finally called in your favor."

"Thank you for meeting us," I said, returning her smile with a dark one of my own. I appreciated that Lyr didn't try to come forward for an embrace. That wasn't my style. Her ability to understand our boundaries was one of the biggest reasons we were still friends. That, and she was smart enough to know having me on her side was an asset.

"Not at all," she said primly, but we both knew I hadn't really left her with a choice. She owed us for standing by her all those years ago when the leaders of the other houses had tried to push her and her mates out. Like us, Lyr didn't like playing by the rules.

Like me and my brothers, Lyr and her males were all different types of monsters, and they should have belonged to other houses, but there was no separating them. When she'd put forward the case that she wanted to create her own lower house, my father had been the only one on the council she couldn't influence.

Lyr was a white tiger shifter and a spy, a good one, and I suspected she'd blackmailed half the council. Those she couldn't blackmail, she'd bribed using riches that had likely come from their own pockets.

My father had been the only one still standing in her way, and that was where I'd come in. I'd known the favor she owed me would be useful one day, but I'd never imagined it would be for this. I was willing to bet neither had she.

"Did you bring what we asked?"

My gaze went to Kade, and he nodded his response, confirming he'd asked for what we'd discussed.

"I'll admit, I was intrigued by your request. Four males asking for female clothing?" One of her brows rose, but I didn't take the bait. Realizing I wasn't going to play, she gestured to Dean. The green monster lifted the case he was carrying and placed it on the table before me. Unclipping the metal clasps, he let the lid fall open.

"I only have three garments I can spare, newly created by my tailors. They have been made to my specifications, but they should do if the female's of a similar size."

I eyed the shiny leather garments neatly folded in the case. Knowing Lyr, they'd likely cost an immense sum and had been crafted using Katakin's top tailor, but they'd be practical. "They'll do. And the vials?"

Her chin tipped upward slightly, but she reached into her pocket and held out three glass vials filled with black blood. "This will buy you time, but only if Warrick doesn't analyze the blood too closely. Otherwise, it'll become obvious this is shifter blood. *My* blood."

Grabbing the vials, I stuffed them into my pocket. "We only need a few nights."

Lyr watched me carefully. "You know you won't be able to hide her for long. Once the week is up, the human will have to compete like all the other newbloods."

I resisted the urge to rub my temple. Kade had agreed not to tell Lyr or her mates anything about Raine and our plans, but I wasn't surprised the tiger shifter had figured it out on her own. Hell, the human's scent was all over the place. "By then, she'll have changed," I said.

"And if she hasn't? You know what this could mean."

I sighed heavily and pinched the bridge of my nose. "We'll deal with that if the time comes."

Lyr's expression became serious. "No one has seen Queen Izla since she slipped through that portal two hundred years ago. When King Adrien went to that island and found only the humans, he'd been on a rampage. It was lucky he'd come to his senses and realized the humans could be useful if they had an agreement. For almost two centuries, we've used the humans as test subjects to check if the curse remained the same. In all that time, the curse has never changed. If the human doesn't turn, there are many who would be interested. And what if the fae find out—"

"There hasn't been a fae attack in years," Darian commented.

"We need to be united if we're to stand a chance," Lyr continued, not deterred by Darian's comment. Her blue gaze sharpened. "The balance is fragile. Between the threat of fae attacks and the appearance of the outlier monsters, there are many who are uncertain. When the monarchy crumbled and the high houses were created and took power, governed by the council, there was at least a sense of peace. That peace can't be upset. Monsters do horrible things when they are afraid."

I slid my gaze to Asher then, worried Lyr's comment might have triggered him to think about his past, but my friend just grinned back at me.

"Lyr, can we rely on you not to say anything?" I asked.

She stared at me as if insulted by my words. "Just be careful who you speak to about the human. Even your father—"

My angry glare was enough to quiet her. "No one will know other than those in this room. Why do you think we require your blood?"

She nodded then, but her brow remained creased. "I need a drink."

Before she'd even turned to the table of spirits, Dean was striding there. He poured both Lyr and himself a drink and placed a silver goblet in Lyr's hands.

"Thanks," she said to her mate with a smile that was so full of genuine happiness that I felt uncomfortable watching them.

The shifter lifted the goblet to her lips. I wanted to ask her about the bond the human had forged among me and my brothers. If anyone had answers, it would be her. Lyr had been Queen Izla's personal spy and knew all sorts of information about monsters and magic. But while she was one of the only other monsters we trusted, we didn't need her knowing that a human could be our destruction.

Lyr downed her drink in one motion and pulled the goblet from her lips. "Well, if that's all, we'd better be on our way," she said, placing the goblet on a nearby table and trailing her nails affectionately over Dean's shoulder. "We left Nic and Soren dealing with a...minor inconvenience. I hope you guys know what you're doing," she purred and strode from the room, Dean close behind her.

CHAPTER 18

~ Raine ~

"You can come out now, Raine dearest," Darian called from the common room.

He didn't need to tell me twice. Now that the white-haired female was gone, I stepped out from where I'd been eavesdropping in Kade's bedroom. The door had been cracked just enough that I was able to snatch glimpses of the female monster they called Lyr, and my stomach had dropped the moment I'd seen her. The monster looked like a goddess with eyes the color of the ocean and pouty pink lips that looked as though they were begging to be kissed.

Releasing a breath, I strode into the common room. "Who was that?" I asked. I'd meant to sound nonchalant, but my words came out clipped.

"A friend," Kade growled.

Friend? I wasn't sure why the thought of this female being their friend left my throat dry. I hated these monsters. Right? My gaze landed on the open case on the table closest to Locke.

Following my gaze, Locke gestured to the case before I could even ask. "Take these," he said. His gaze swung to the right, landing on one of the iron doors. "Washroom's through there."

I eyed the door but didn't move. "First, explain what you were talking about with that female. What did she mean when she said I have to compete?"

Locke's eyes narrowed to slits, the whites disappearing, and a dark energy crackled through the room. "Clothes first. No one can concentrate when you're standing there half-naked."

I bit my tongue to stop myself from arguing and glared at him. From his hard gaze, I knew he wasn't going to take no for an answer, and if I refused, it wouldn't have surprised me if he'd forced me into the washroom himself.

Cursing him under my breath, I strode over and surveyed the items in the case. Three garments were neatly folded, one red and two black, and all made of the finest leather I'd ever seen. I grabbed the red one in the middle and held it up, letting the material unfurl.

The leather top had a low *V* in the chest and tapered off to a small waist. I raised a brow at the low *V* but didn't comment. Anything was better than this shirt.

The next item was a pair of red trousers. The leather was so shiny I could see the outline of my face. They'd be slightly on the short side, but otherwise, they looked to be the right size.

A glimpse of lacy black material was hidden under one of the outfits, and I dug my fingers into the case, pulling it out and holding up... *Lacy black panties?* Well, I couldn't fault Lyr for packing an entire outfit. She'd even packed two pairs of boots, one red and one black, which were folded at the bottom of the case.

"Thank you, Lyr," Asher muttered behind me, but I didn't give him the satisfaction of a reaction.

I didn't care if the panties were lacy, nor did I care if Locke had specifically requested them or not. At least I had some.

Snatching up the outfit, I ignored the monsters who watched me and disappeared through the doorway that Locke had indicated led to the washroom.

Closing the door behind me, I spun to face the room, and my jaw dropped open. The space was even larger than Kade's room. Blue torches flared to life up high on the walls, and a round pool was spread before me, taking up the majority of the space.

The sparkling blue water glittered, shining beautiful patterns on the stone walls. In the middle of the pool, water rushed out from a hole in the ceiling, spraying down, reminding me of the spray from a waterfall.

A mirror spread across the wall on the left, and a rack containing stacked towels was neatly pressed against the opposite wall. A small door sat at the far back, and I guessed it led to the water closet.

Mother, pinch me.

Dropping my new red outfit onto a stone shelf, I began to undress. When I was standing naked, I eyed the water. Locke had only ordered me to get changed, but it had been so long since I'd properly bathed, and I still had sand rubbing in places I didn't want to think about from when the rocky ceiling had turned to sand.

Fuck it. If they're going to make me wait for answers, they can wait too. I stepped down the stone steps that led into the pool and groaned as I sank into the crystal water, the warmth of the liquid soothing my bruised body.

Swimming to the middle, I stood, letting the spray from the ceiling run down my face and stream down my hair. Closing my eyes, I enjoyed the feel of the water rushing over my body, washing away the grime of the past few nights. For the briefest moment, it was as if I could wash away the memories. As if I was back on my island, away from all of this. I'd often bathed in the spray of waterfalls on the island, and this was just as good. No, it was *better*. I sighed. *But you still haven't found Cara.* The thought speared through my feeling of bliss, leaving the dark stain of guilt. I didn't have time for this. What was I doing?

I waded from the water and grabbed one of the plush black towels, drying myself off.

Idle chatter and laughter came from the common room, but for once, I wasn't paying attention to what they said. When I was dry, I slid into the supple leather outfit left by the monster Lyr and peered at myself in the mirror.

I hardly recognized my reflection. The leather fitted tightly to me like a second skin, molding to every groove of my body, accentuating my thin waist and hugging tightly to my ass. The deep *V* of the top curved downward, revealing a healthy dose of cleavage. *All right, ladies, I know it's a squeeze, but it's the best we've got*, I mused internally, consoling my breasts.

Aside from being tight in the chest, the outfit fitted nicely. I looked...*badass*. The red leather was a vast improvement to the white dress I'd been wearing when I first arrived. I wasn't sure how Locke thought this would be less of a distraction than the shirt, but that wasn't my problem.

Smirking at my reflection, I raked my fingers through my wet strands of red-brown hair. *Definitely an improvement.* There were even hidden pockets around my ribcage, clearly designed for holding various blades and weapons. *Lyr is my kind of girl.* I instantly had a newfound respect for the female.

I finished the outfit with the pair of red boots and sauntered into the common room. I hadn't really intended to sway my hips from side to side, but it was as if this outfit demanded I do it justice.

I'd barely made it a few steps from the door when four pairs of eyes were on me, watching me walk across the room.

Asher let out a low, appreciative whistle, his gaze trailing down my body and lingering on my cleavage. "Locke, you sure lettin' her borrow Lyr's outfit was a good idea? I'm not sure it fits."

Heat rushed to my cheeks, but I kept my back straight.

Darian's lips curved upward into a sensual smile. "Lyr always has had good taste."

"Would you have preferred I leave her in Kade's shirt?" Locke questioned.

Asher shrugged his broad shoulders and grinned mischievously. "I'm just sayin' if you thought this was going to be less distractin', you were mistaken."

"I think he just wanted her to put some pants on," Darian commented with wry amusement.

I slid my gaze to Kade, half expecting him to comment about being glad to have his shirt back, but the wolf monster just stared at me, his serious gaze burning down the length of my body.

"Thanks," I said earnestly, forcing my gaze away from Kade's golden eyes and to Locke. I had a feeling he was the one responsible for the outfit, and I was grateful. I'd been starting to think the shirt was the best I was going to get.

"For what?" Locke said, his dark gaze unreadable as he watched me.

For being decent and offering me panties? "For the clothes," I said.

His gaze remained fixed on me. "Couldn't have you walking around in Kade's shirts for the next few nights."

"She could've borrowed some of mine," Asher piped up, but Locke ignored him.

I shifted under Locke's gaze. "Right." I cleared my throat. "Well, I'm dressed. Now it's your turn. What the hell did Lyr mean when she said I will still have to compete?"

Locke studied me, and for a moment, I didn't think he would respond, but then he said, "By the end of the week, all the newly changed are to compete in the Week of Orash."

"The week of what?"

"The Week of Orash is when it's determined what house you will belong to. All monsters belong to a house. There are the main powerful high houses and then dozens of lower houses. For example, there is the House of Nesarin, the high house of vampires, but there are also vampires who have grouped to create lower houses."

"The newbloods fight each other and prance around at parties, hoping to catch the eye of their respective high house," Darian added, his tone sounding bored. "The higher houses have more influence, more money."

"So you four all belong to different houses?"

From their answering frowns and stares, I guessed I'd touched on a sore spot.

"That's not your concern," Locke answered me.

My brow creased as I tried to understand what they were talking about. *They let the newbloods join houses? Will Cara be watching during the Week of Orash?*

My thoughts then went to the other villagers who had been chosen alongside me. I hadn't seen any of them since we were first separated after coming to this place, and the idea of seeing them again was a relief. *But they're not human anymore*, I reminded myself. "But what if I haven't turned into a monster by then?" I asked.

Locke's dark brows slammed down. "From now on, you're to pretend you're a shifter like Kade and Lyr. When you do finally change, if you turn into something else, we can pretend you mustn't have fully turned before, and so we just suspected shifter blood. It's not an ideal situation, but it should keep the Taratun at bay for now."

"But what if a house offers to let me join them?" I had no intention of letting it get that far. I'd escape before then. Parties and fighting? It sounded like there would be a lot of distractions going on, and if ever there was a time to escape and find Cara, it would be then. But I wasn't an idiot. I needed to think through all possible situations.

"Let's hope we can find a way to sever the bond before then."

A sharp pang went through me. I knew they only cared about two things: the fact the bond with me endangered their lives and the fact me not turning into a monster threatened the peace of their hellish kingdom. But hearing those words still stung.

"And if we can't?" I asked.

"We'll worry about that later. Tomorrow night, we'll continue testing you and trying to bring on the change. I suggest you get some rest."

I wanted to protest. To demand he answer my questions until this damn world started making more sense. It was clearly way more complex than just monsters turning humans into them. The monsters were organized.

The basics of what I understood so far were that the fact I hadn't changed into a monster was unusual, and by the end of the week I'd be forced to participate in the Week of Orash and fight those from my village.

"Kade, she'll sleep with you. I don't trust Dar and Ash with her, and I have an errand to run before I can call it a day."

Sleep with him? "Uh, excuse me, but I'm not sleeping with anyone," I interjected.

"And don't touch her," Locke added as if he thought this would appease me.

I glowered at Locke, then turned to the golden-eyed male, who was standing so rigid my muscles ached just from looking at him. Throwing my hands in the air at the lot of them, I stormed into Kade's room. *Fucking monsters.*

CHAPTER 19

~ **Raine** ~

Kade followed me into his bedroom, and I tried not to think about his hulking figure at my back.

Halfway across the room, I stopped before the massive bed. A new woolen blanket rested on top as if someone had changed the linen since I'd last been in there. The idea of crawling beneath the blanket onto the wolf monster's ultrasoft bed seemed heavenly, but if I had my way, I wouldn't be sleeping at all.

"This is ridiculous," I said, turning to him. "I can find somewhere to sleep in the main room."

Kade's look was deadpan as if he was as pleased about this as I was and I was wasting his time. "Bed," he said in that growly voice of his.

I narrowed my eyes. "And where will you sleep?"

In response to my question, he reached back to grab his shirt with one hand and pulled it over his head, revealing a torso of hard, perfect abs that rippled as he moved. Striding to the left side of the bed, he lifted the blanket and jumped onto the mattress. Draping the blanket back over himself, he folded his thick arms behind his head and closed his eyes.

I gaped. *Unbelievable.* Shifting uncomfortably, I weighed my options. There was plenty of room on the other side of the bed. Enough that even with me sleeping near the edge, there would still be four feet between us. I thought of crawling onto the mattress to sleep next Kade—the same wolf monster who had almost killed me not long ago.

I should have hated him, and I did, but...he'd also saved me. Even if he'd thought we were bonded and his life was linked to mine, he'd made the choice not to let me bleed to death. And even now, it was as if something was pulling me toward him. Telling me to move closer to him.

I glanced to where the blanket wasn't high enough to cover his broad chest. Would he stay on his side of the bed? I remembered the searing pain as his wolf fangs had buried into my thigh, and then the image of his naked human body appeared in my mind. The male was raw masculinity, rough and untamed, and my body reacted to the thought of his on mine.

Warmth pooled in my core, and I swallowed. *Sleeping with the enemy will not help you find Cara*, I chastised myself, squashing the thought of his huge... *Fuck, Raine. Pull it together.*

Kade's nostrils flared as if he was scenting the air, and my heart rate quickened. Did the monster know what I was thinking?

Oh, hell no. In a few strides, I was at the side of the bed. I yanked the huge blanket off in one swift movement and snatched up the closest pillow. Kade watched me with one eye cracked, but he said nothing as I exposed him to the cool air.

Throwing the blanket to the floor, I folded it over so I could crawl between it and rested my head on the pillow. It wasn't exactly comfortable, especially not in the tight leather outfit, and I momentarily wished I was back wearing Kade's shirt, but there was no way I was stripping, and I'd slept on worse.

I grinned, somehow feeling triumphant, but then my face sobered as I realized I was proud of myself for not jumping into bed with a monster. *What an achievement.* I sighed. I was in trouble.

· · · ● · ● · · ·

It was a long time before the bastard fell asleep. I lay on the floor motionless until the steady rhythm of Kade's breathing filled the room, the only sound in the otherwise silent space. No sounds came from the common room either. I continued to wait for what felt like another hour, and then I slid from the blanket cocoon I'd made.

The only light came from a lone blue torch burning near the door, and I padded slowly around in the dark until I came to the desk that rested against the wall opposite the door.

The polished wood surface was bare except for an ink pen, a blank piece of paper, and a letter opener. Grabbing the letter opener, I tested the pointed tip against my finger. It was blunted, of course, but it could still work as a weapon if I pressed hard enough.

My fingers trailed to one of the two drawers underneath the right side of the desk. I bit my lip and cringed at the low scraping sound as I opened the first drawer, turning to watch Kade. The monster's broad chest continued to rise and fall steadily, and I let out the breath I'd been holding. *Thank the Goddess.*

My deft fingers searched through the contents of the drawer—blank paper, a bottle of ink, and a stick of wax. Frowning, I closed the drawer and opened the second drawer just as carefully as I had the first. A bunch of reports were neatly stacked, and I picked through them eagerly. Since I'd come to this place, this was the first time I'd found something that might actually give me information.

Lifting the stack of paper from the drawer, I rested it on the table and scanned the first page. I swallowed as I stared at the picture of a dead human that was pasted to the left of the page. *No, not dead. Bri.* Bri's chestnut-colored hair lay lifeless around her head, but I knew it was her. The girl from the lineup with me. If Locke and the others were telling the truth, then in this picture she was likely unconscious, not dead. This report had to be from the past few nights.

Bri was sprawled on a cot, similar to the one I'd slept on when I'd first come to this place, and she was dressed in her dirty white garment.

I turned my attention to the rest of the page and began reading. It didn't take me long to realize what I was looking at. *Day 1: The human subject is already showing signs of the change. From analyzing her blood sample, it can be concluded the curse will take her in the next 24 hours.*

Subconsciously, I rubbed the inside of my right arm. *So that's why Locke asked for the vials of blood from Lyr.* The thought that someone had been coming to collect my blood all this time made me shiver.

I scanned the rest of the page. There were details on Bri's reactions in the first two trials. She'd changed during the second trial with the rocks falling from the ceiling. Another picture was at the bottom of the page, and in this one, Bri was staring straight forward, green horns protruding from her chestnut-colored hair and green eyes staring back at me. *She's a demon.*

Kade shifted on the bed behind me, and I quickly glanced his way. When the male didn't stir, I began rifling through the other pages. They were all there. The other villagers.

I searched through them quickly, knowing Kade could wake at any moment. When I reached the bottom of the stack, I paused. My report wasn't there. Neither were any from the previous trials. I sighed, trying to contain my disappointment. *Cara's report isn't here.*

Turning my attention back to the drawer, I noticed a silky black piece of cardboard that had been left on the bottom, the border edged with intricate golden swirls. Carefully, I pulled it out, lifting the paper closer to my face so I could make out the small writing in white.

You are cordially invited to attend the Week of Orash... I read the words in my mind. There were specific dates, which meant nothing to me, as they didn't coincide with the way we'd counted the days back on the island, and the mention of a location.

Kade shifted behind me, and I hastily placed the papers back in the drawer, arranging them how I'd found them, and closed the drawer as quietly as I could. All the while, I couldn't stop thinking about how fucked up the whole situation was. They weren't just turning the people from my island into monsters. They expected us to just accept it and become part of their world.

My stomach churned, and my thoughts turned to Cara. She was only sixteen when she'd been taken and forced to go through this. *And it's all my fault.* My hands shook. I knew something was happening to me. The monsters had told me I would change into something, more than once, but I didn't really care about that. I was here for Cara.

As my guilt crushed me, my anger rose. Fury was the only thing that kept me going. It was my fault she'd been taken early, but if it weren't for these monsters, there wouldn't be an offering at all. Without them, Cara and I would still be on the island, happily living our lives.

I gripped the letter opener in my hand and stalked toward the bed. Toward the monster who was still sleeping, his breathing steady as if he was in a deep slumber. Toward the monster who had reports of the newly turned in his drawer. The one who'd nearly killed me by letting his wolf sink his teeth into my thigh. A small part of my brain tried to remind me he'd also saved my life, but I wasn't thinking about that. All I was picturing was Cara's thin frame as she was led into the mouth of Procus back on the island.

In his sleep, Kade had rolled further into the middle of the bed, but he still rested on his back with his arms up near his head. I crawled onto the bed and lifted my leg over him, straddling him without letting my weight rest on him.

I held the letter opener before me, the tool hovering in the air, poised above his neck. The steel of the letter opener was thin and flimsy and didn't at all have the weight of a dagger, but it still rested perfectly in my palm.

I glared at the sleeping monster. *He's been a part of it.* I couldn't be sure he'd had a part in Cara's fate here, but he certainly did with the villagers who'd been chosen alongside me. I'd been a fool. It was only now that I realized I'd started to trust them. I'd started to think of them as more than the monsters they were. *Fucking idiot.*

Kade's face was relaxed, the lines smoothed on his forehead. Damn it, he appeared so human. So handsome. Not at all like the beast I'd run from in the cavern. *You can do this, Raine. He's not human. Just a monster.* My hand trembled. The magic that bound us was still pulling me toward him. Telling me he was safe. That I should get close to him. Repelling me against killing him.

Fuck. I fought against the feelings and drove the letter opener down, aiming the tip of the object at the male's jugular. Before the steel could push into the flesh of his neck, Kade's eyes snapped open, and his hand flew up to clutch my wrist, suspending the letter opener just above his skin. Anger flared in his gaze, but he didn't react.

I pushed against him, trying to drive the letter opener down, but his grip was like iron. His hand tightened on my wrist and moved my arm to the side so the letter opener was no longer above his neck. Gritting my teeth, I tried to shuffle my body backward, away from him, but the monster's other huge hand gripped my ass, holding me in place above him.

The pain in my wrist became strong enough that my eyes began to water. Reluctantly, I opened my hand, releasing the letter opener. It landed with a soft thud on the bed beside Kade. *Fucker.*

The pair of us stared at each other, his glowing golden gaze searing into mine. I stayed still, hardly daring to breathe. I knew I'd done it now. This was *definitely* a death sentence. But then again, they thought they couldn't kill me, right?

But Kade didn't snap my neck or throw me across the room. I squirmed as he continued to hold me tight, not giving me an inch to move. The longer I was stuck there, the more I became increasingly aware of my position.

I'd thought it was a great idea at the time, but now here I was, perched above him like some forlorn lover. Worse, the longer I stayed there staring at those golden eyes, the more the pull I had toward him cut through my anger, the magic clouding my thoughts, my feelings.

I swallowed as Kade's other hand gripped my ass more firmly, like he was trying to dig his fingers into the leather. Where his rounded ears had been, they were now pointed as if his wolf was trying to break through. I had the distinct thought that I was like a rabbit who had walked into a predator's line of sight, but I squashed the thought quickly. I wasn't a fucking rabbit. Kade's intense gaze trailed from my face to where I was seated on him, and his frown deepened.

I tried not to think about it. Tried not to think about the way that golden gaze made me feel. Like I was completely exposed but completely safe at the same time. *Ha! Safe.* The word made me want to laugh out loud, but I couldn't deny the feeling.

Somehow, I *knew* that even though I'd just tried to kill him, this monster, this male, wouldn't kill me. The hardness of his body between my thighs felt too right, and my body responded.

I hated him. Hated *them.* But my body disagreed. It wanted them, and the pull toward him was getting too strong. But I couldn't. I could *not* do this. *I fucking hate them.*

"Let me go," I snarled.

In a swift movement, the male flipped me off him and slammed my back onto the bed, and then he was on me, one hand pinning my wrists above my head.

"Asshole," I hissed.

His head dipped, his nose trailing along the side of my face. The huge male breathed in deeply and puffed out, his breath warming my face.

Did he just fucking smell me? "Did you just—?"

"What did you do to us, human?" he growled, cutting me off. His mouth trailed closer to my ear again. "And why is my wolf urging me to fuck you when he should want to rip your head off?"

I opened my mouth to speak but then closed it again. Wetness pooled between my thighs. *He wants to fuck me?* Well, technically he'd said his *wolf* wanted to, but they were the same person, right?

When I didn't answer, he lifted his leg and rubbed his thigh against my core. "Funny that you try to kill me but at the same time, your panties are soaked."

"I do—"

He ground his leg against me, and my words were cut off as I forced myself to hold back the moan that threatened to escape me.

"I do want to kill you," I finally managed to say through gritted teeth.

Kade's thigh stilled between my legs. His muscles were trembling, but he pulled away from me, releasing my hands and sitting up on the bed. "Then you'd better get the fuck up. Let's go before my wolf has his way."

Scrambling to the side of the bed, I shot to my feet, staring at Kade's broad back as he picked up his shirt from the floor and pulled it on.

"Go where?"

"You'll see."

CHAPTER 20

~ Kade ~

I clenched my jaw, internally fighting my wolf for control. He'd never been like this before. Wild. Feral. *Desperate.* Even in the beginning, when we'd been just starting to get to know each other, he'd never fought so hard against me.

I quickened my pace, not caring that Raine was almost running to keep up. It was her fault this was happening. Whatever she'd done to us, however she'd bonded us, my wolf believed she was his. I'd felt his primal satisfaction when we'd been in my bed, my leg grinding against her, the scent of her arousal driving us both mad. He didn't care that she'd tried to end our life.

I cursed Locke for making me watch her. I was supposed to be the safe option, and here I was, frantic to get to the training ground, my cock so hard in my pants it ached. All because of that female. That *human* who wanted me dead.

It was a relief when I reached the iron double doors of the training cavern. Turning, I waited for her. When she stopped beside me, her body looking way too fuckable in that bloody leather outfit Lyr had provided for her, I opened the doors. When we were both through, I shut them again and scoured the area quickly to check it was empty, then I jogged straight for the massive obstacle course at the other end of the cavern.

I'd told my brothers I'd keep her in our shared space, but if I'd stayed there, who knows what would have happened. It was the middle of the day outside of the mountain, so odds were most of the monsters were asleep. Either way, I was taking my chances. Besides, I had a feeling Raine needed this as much as I did.

With her scent still in my nostrils from where she stood at the other end of the room, I raced through the obstacle course faster than ever before, leaping across spaces, climbing over walls higher than houses, scaling up and down the ropes that dangled from the ceiling, and running and dodging like a crazed animal. I knew she was watching. Her scent of coconut and steel permeated the air like it was determined to be known.

By the time I'd completed the course three times, sweat streamed from me, soaking my hair and shirt. I was still hard, but my wolf had settled a little. Enough for me to control him, at least.

If the human weren't with me, I would have let him run out his frustration using his own paws, but I couldn't trust him when he was like this. Hungry. Insatiable. Not with her around. Even if she weren't there, I couldn't have been sure he wouldn't hunt her down, no matter where she went in the mountain.

I strode back toward the human, who was busy inspecting the racks of weapons against one wall. She pretended not to notice me, but her eyes slid to the side, watching as I grabbed a towel and wiped off my face. I guzzled water from a nearby jug and ripped off my sweaty shirt.

I detected the scent of the human's arousal, and I couldn't stop the low growl that rumbled out of me.

"You're up," I said, stalking over to her.

"What?"

"You heard me. Get moving," I said, gesturing to the obstacle course with my head.

Her eyes grew wide, but she didn't argue. "Fine."

I wasn't surprised she agreed. This human wasn't like the others. The whole time she'd been watching me, I could feel her excitement at the sight of the challenge. She *wanted* to try the obstacle course.

And I was right. Raine was born to run, and she raced through the obstacles like they were made for her. She was nowhere near as fast as most monsters, but I admired her determination. Admired the way she would size up the obstacle, calculating the best way to conquer it before tackling it without an ounce of fear. This wasn't a course made for humans, but she was doing a damn good job.

My shouts and growls from the sideline spurred her to go faster until her face was red and fatigue pulled at her features. Increased stress and a rapid heartbeat were supposed to make the change happen faster for humans, and she really needed to fucking change, so I pushed her harder. The sooner her blood turned black, the better it would be for my brothers and me, and for her.

I couldn't fucking protect her, no matter how much the bond was compelling me to do so. Her best chance was to turn so she wouldn't be a target. The human was about to swing on a rope across a deep pit when the faint sound of chatter had my head turning toward the door.

My nostrils flared, and in a few strides, I was by Raine's side, grasping her shoulder to stop her from grabbing the rope.

"What the hell?" she snapped.

I silenced her by clamping my hand over her mouth. "Quiet. They'll hear you," I said low into her ear.

Immediately, she stilled.

I gestured my head to the narrow stairway on the left side of the cavern. At the top stood a narrow iron door. "See that door?"

Her gaze slid to where I was gesturing, and she nodded.

"It leads to a balcony. Fliers use it to access the training cavern when they're outside of the mountain. Go there and shut the door behind you. I'll collect you when it's clear."

To my relief, she didn't question me.

"Run," I added as I released her.

Jumping down from the platform we'd been on, I strode toward the middle of the cavern. I knew who was coming before he even stepped through the doors. There was no mistaking that voice, that scent. *Zacal and his wolves.*

Peering back, I noted where Raine was still climbing the stairs. *Faster*, I willed her in my mind. *Fuck.* She'd been sweating all over the place. If Zacal caught her, I wasn't sure what he'd try to do. I just hoped she was smart enough to stay hidden.

I turned forward again as Zacal strode into the room, an arrogant smirk on his face. His three most loyal wolves were with him. Wolves who had once been loyal to me before all the shit that had gone down.

The moment Zacal spotted me standing in the middle of the room, sadistic delight sparked in his eyes, and I rolled my neck. He wasn't going to make this easy. He never did. And I welcomed the pain.

· · · ● · ● · · ·

~ **Raine** ~

My legs and chest burned by the time I reached the top of the staircase. Swiftly, I pulled the narrow iron door open and stepped through, sighing as frigid mountain air cooled my hot cheeks and a chill breeze teased my unbound hair. My heart leaped at the realization that for the first time since I'd come to this place, I was *outside*.

Closing the door, I squinted against the sunlight that speared from above, my eyes watering. After numerous blinks, I made out the small balcony I stood on, which was carved from a wide rock shelf jutting out of the mountain. An intricate marble railing lined the edge, clearly designed to stop anyone from accidentally falling to their deaths.

I strained my eyes, searching the expanse of blue above, but no flying monsters came swooping down on me. *Fliers*, Kade had called them. *Thank the Goddess monsters sleep during the day.*

Stepping forward, I moved to the edge of the balcony and stifled a gasp. Far below at the base of the mountain, rows upon rows of buildings spread before me, rivers of glowing blue winding between the stone houses, like tentacles reaching for the ocean. In the center of it all, silver-tipped stone towers reached into the sky.

I stared, overwhelmed by what I was seeing. *Holy Mother Falia, there must be hundreds of thousands of monsters. How am I supposed to find Cara in that?* Making my way through the tunnels of the mountain was already a difficult task, but finding her in all that seemed impossible. Clenching my jaw, I forced myself not to think about it. *First, escape. You can tackle that problem after.*

I turned my attention to the rocky mountainside around the balcony. A thin shelf of rock led off on the right side, connecting to another small balcony further around the mountain. The path was narrow but possibly just large enough that I could shuffle my way along if I was careful.

Wiping my forehead with the back of my hand, I steeled myself and stepped toward the edge of the balcony. *Don't look down. Don't you fucking dare look down.* Resting my palms on the balcony railing, I took a deep breath and mentally prepared myself for what I was about to do. Before I moved forward, a low howl mixed with the wind, and I frowned as I wondered at the sound. *You're up high. It's just the wind playing tricks.*

Dismissing the noise, I lifted my leg and gripped the railing harder. As I was about to hoist myself over another howl rang out. I paused. The sound was deep, guttural, and so full of agony that my gut tightened, my throat becoming dry. *Kade.*

I stared at my path to freedom. *Don't you dare turn around. This is your chance. Cara's chance. Who cares if the monster asshole is in danger? He's a big boy. He can take care of himself.* I chewed the inside of my cheek. I should have been escaping. I came here for Cara. It was all that mattered, but I didn't move. Another of Kade's howls cut through the wind, and the bond between us wrapped around me, making my chest squeeze.

Shit. I cursed at myself, my face scrunching in frustration, and spun around, stepping back toward the door. Letting out a heavy breath through my nose, I cracked open the door and peered down into the training cavern.

Kade was crouched, an arm resting on his knee and the other knee on the ground, the muscles of his shoulder pronounced beneath his shirt. A long stripe of black reached across his back, and my brows lowered as I took in the blood. Three males and a female stood around him, each with a weapon brandished in their hand. Their faces were full of so much rage and glee that it made my lip curl.

Get up, Kade. What the hell is going on?

"Stop holding out on us, Kade. We know you have a newblood hiding here somewhere. Her scent is all over the cavern," said the broadest of the three males, his voice like gravel. "All we want is a taste." The male was a head shorter than Kade, with copper eyes and brown hair shaved close to his head. A long blade hung at his side, glistening with black blood. *Kade's blood.*

I tensed, feeling the adrenaline surge through me. *They're looking for me.* I swallowed. *Well, good. Kade deserves whatever these monsters have to give. Now move your ass while they're distracted.* My gaze flitted to the edge of the balcony and the rocky shelf that was my chance of escape, but I hesitated. *You hate him, remember? The fucker bit you.*

Except...he'd also saved me. Even if he thought our lives were linked by whatever the hell the bond was, he'd saved me and hadn't been cruel. He *hadn't* acted like a monster. And the thought of him being hurt because they were looking for me left a sour taste in my mouth. *Come on, Kade, you're a big badass. You can take those monsters.*

I didn't really know if he could. There were four of them and one of him, and I had no idea what kind of monsters the others were, but Kade was a huge wall of muscle, and from the way he tore around the obstacle course, he was fit as hell.

"There's no one else here, and we both know you're more interested in me," Kade said, his voice already sounding defeated.

I gritted my teeth. *No, get up and fight!*

"To think you should have been the alpha," said the short-haired monster who I guessed was the leader. "The strongest wolf alpha of Katakin." The male scoffed. "A wolf who couldn't even protect his family."

Wait, what? I waited for Kade to react, but he didn't move from his half-kneeling position and kept his head bowed. Another one of the monsters, the female with her dark hair tied in a high bun, snarled and left another stripe of black on his back.

Kade only grunted at the pain.

The short-haired male laughed, and a vicious smile curved his thin lips. "Look at you. You're pathetic. No wonder you couldn't protect them. You're weak."

"You weren't there when they needed you!" another one of the males shouted, and as I tried to piece together what they were saying, my heart began to ache for Kade. About what they implied happened to his family.

Kade, Locke, Asher, and Darian hadn't mentioned anything about having a family. Not that I'd bothered to ask. Why would I?

"I won't fight you, Zacal." Kade's voice was a low growl, and the pull of our bond urged me to move toward him.

"When the fae came, do you think your mother and sister believed you would save them? Or do you think they knew you were too busy with your...*friends* to care about the pack? To care about *them.*"

His mother and sister? Dread filled me. From the way Kade refused to fight or even respond to the other monster's taunts, it was obvious he blamed himself for whatever had happened. *He thinks it was his fault.*

Annoyance crossed the monster Zacal's face when Kade still didn't respond. The male signaled with his hand, and his followers started forward, attacking Kade without mercy. They struck him with their blades, anger twisting their features, as I watched on.

The pit in my stomach grew, but Kade remained where he was, taking the onslaught. Zacal lunged, and his sword sliced toward Kade's face, slashing along his left cheek. Kade's head turned to the side with the force, and black blood flicked to the stone floor.

Fucking get up! I wanted to grab Kade's shoulders and shake him. To break him out of whatever trance he was in. Whether he was responsible for whatever happened with his family or not, this was all wrong. And I couldn't stand to watch it unfold.

I clenched and unclenched my fists at my side. I knew I should close the door, ignore them, and leg it out of there, but as much as I told myself I hated Kade, what I really hated was this whole situation. I hated that Cara was taken. I hated that it was partially my fault. And I hated that the monsters were turning us into them and stealing our lives from us.

But... Kade wasn't responsible for all that. I couldn't be sure how much he *was* responsible for, but no one deserved to be sliced to death. And especially not if they were grieving. I didn't know what had happened, but what I did know was that he didn't need these assholes to torture him. He was clearly already torturing himself. And from how I'd seen Kade act with Locke and the others, I couldn't help but feel like these monsters weren't telling the full story of what had happened.

Can monsters die? I'd wondered this since stabbing Asher in the shoulder and seeing him heal instantly. But

Kade wasn't healing like the monster with the violet horns. *Fuck.*

Before I could second-guess myself, I swung open the door and flew down the steps, two at a time. *Please don't let this get me killed.*

Halfway down the staircase, I shouted, "Leave him alone, assholes!"

Since the monsters were consumed by the frenzy, it took a moment before they stopped, but then their unwelcome gazes shot my way, narrowing on me as I made my way down the last of the steps.

Kade's golden gaze connected with mine, and fear flickered in the depths, his eyes widening. Blood dripped from him, including from a deep gash that had been carved into his right arm. Something inside me twisted at the sight of his beautiful body marred so cruelly.

"What do we have here?" Zacal said with a wicked grin. His yellow gaze became hungry as he stared at me, and I suppressed my shudder.

"She has nothing to do with this," Kade said, slowly rising to his feet.

I didn't take my eyes off Zacal. He was the biggest threat, and I still had no idea what abilities he had.

"Leave Kade alone," I said coldly, repeating myself as I reached the bottom of the stairs. "He's carrying out the Taratun's wishes."

Before I could reach Kade, Zacal stepped between us, his expression turning appreciative as his gaze slid up and down my body, blatantly admiring me. "Is he now?" Zacal said, his top lip lifting, showing pointed fangs.

I glared at him and kept my chin high. "The Taratun sent us here to train for the Week of Orash now that I've turned, but we were supposed to be back a while ago." I had no idea if what I was saying sounded believable, but it was the only excuse I could think of.

Zacal's copper eyes narrowed. "Training for the Week of Orash?" He lifted his head, his nostrils flaring as he sniffed the air. "You smell way too delicious for a newblood. How about I *train* you instead? Show you what it's like with a real alpha."

My stomach churned at the desire swirling in the male's eyes. *How about hell no, asshole.* I smiled sweetly. "Thanks, but no thanks." I stepped around the male and went to Kade's side.

"Told you to hide," Kade muttered under his breath.

"Why do people always think I'll listen?" I quipped quietly back.

I peered at where Kade stood, bleeding all over the floor. Shadows clung to his eyes, and his gaze seemed...empty. "Stay behind me," he said.

I raised a brow at him in disbelief. It was a freaking wonder he was even standing. "How about you stand behind me."

Kade growled in protest and attempted to step in front of me, but I shuffled to the side, and he stumbled, only just managing to stay upright. Like hell was I letting him block my view.

"Well, isn't this sweet," Zacal jeered. "The newblood is trying to protect our shamed alpha from the real wolves of this city."

Real wolves? Something told me this male was spewing bullshit. At least I knew what they were now. "Got a blade?" I whispered to Kade as I eyed the wolf monsters who had moved to surround us.

"No," Kade replied.

I licked my lips nervously. "Not to worry, I'll figure something out."

"Let them have me. I'm not worth it."

"As much as I shouldn't care whether they cut you to ribbons, leaving a damsel in distress isn't something I do anymore." After Cara, I'd vowed I'd never hide from monsters again. That if it came to it, I'd always try to save my loved ones, no matter the cost. Kade wasn't a loved one. Hell, I didn't even like the ass, but I couldn't watch while monsters cut him down. It brought the painful memory of Cara being taken too close to the surface of my mind. I still didn't know where she was, but I knew Kade needed my help now, whether he wanted it or not. It felt right to be *doing* something. I'd felt powerless since coming to this place, but now was my chance to help. To fight. Someone had to.

"Damsel?"

Using my peripheral vision, I eyed the wall of blades and weaponry to the left side of the cavern. There was no way I'd make it. Not with the reflexes of these monsters. If they were as fast as Kade had been when his wolf had chased me, I'd be torn apart before I reached the closest sword.

"Last chance, newblood. You're new here, so I can excuse you for speaking out of step. Let us have our fun with Kade here, and we'll leave you be. You can think of this as your first lesson on how our world works." Zacal smiled, though it looked more like a grimace, his lips tight and teeth bared.

"If this is how your world works, I'd rather make my own rules," I responded, giving him a twisted smile of my own.

Zacal's eyes darkened, and he turned to his followers. "Let's show this newblood how wolves from the House of Worzel treat traitors of the pack, shall we?" He paused and stared me down. "And those who stand with them," he added. "Kasey, the newblood is yours. The rest of us will take care of the traitor."

The female wolf monster fixed her pale-gray eyes on me, and she smiled, a cold sadistic smile. "Yes, boss."

Right. So Kade's too weak to be an alpha, but all three of the males are going to fight him while he's already bleeding out? Sounds fair. I wanted to laugh at the irony of it, but if anything, I knew this was going to work in my favor. They underestimated me. Probably thought I was the typical newblood with no combat training.

Howls erupted from the wolf monsters, and the hairs stood up on the back of my neck. This was nothing like fighting my makeshift monsters, the trees back on the island.

Shit was about to get real. I'd spent my whole life training to fight the Katakin monsters, and here I was, about to find out if my training was good enough. I had the brief thought that I might die, but I dismissed it, clearing my mind and focusing on the movements and sounds of the monsters around me. I could feel the wolves coming closer, Zacal and the other males moving toward Kade while the female, Kasey, stared at me with an assessing gaze.

My heart thudded wildly in my chest and sweat beaded on my brow. Zacal's feet shifted slightly, and then he lunged, his sword arching through the air and his face contorted into an angry scowl. As if that was a signal, the other wolves moved into action, shooting forward as well.

I darted out of the way as Kasey's blade sliced the air where my side had just been.

A grunt sounded behind me, and I turned to see Kade had dodged Zacal's blade only to step into the path of another of the male's swords. The blade cleaved deep into his arm. Kade was fighting, but he was moving too sluggishly, reacting too slowly. Pain haunted his eyes.

"Fight!" I shouted at him as I dodged Kasey's sword again. Spinning around, I shot my foot out, kicking her wrist and sending her blade clattering to the floor to our right. Her eyes narrowed to slits as she glared at me, anger burning in her gaze.

As I watched in horror, her face shifted, elongating to a snout, bared fangs protruding from her mouth and her ears becoming pointed. She bent over as gray fur sprouted over her skin, and her clothes tore as her limbs and torso began to shift, a growl ripping from her throat.

I didn't wait to see the end result. Turning from her, I sprinted toward her blade and jumped to the ground, falling to my belly on the cold stone floor. The scrape of claws on stone sounded behind me, and I knew she was close. The moment my fingers wrapped around the steel hilt of the sword, I flipped onto my back and lifted the blade with a cry of my own.

My arms nearly buckled at the weight of the gray wolf as she impaled herself on the sword, the blade going through her furry neck and a sharp whine escaping her mouth. Blood spurted onto my face, and I heaved, using all my strength to push the wolf off me to fall onto the ground beside me.

Climbing to my feet while still holding the hilt of the sword, I drove the blade in deeper, swallowing the bile that began to rise in my throat. The wolf continued snapping her jaws despite the blood leaking from her and spilling onto the ground. Her powerful paws scraped at the floor, leaving deep grooves in the stone.

The wound would have killed any ordinary animal, but nothing about these monsters was normal. My face blanched at the thought of what I had to do. Surely the monsters would die if they had no head.

I rested my booted foot on the wolf's side and yanked the blade out. Lifting the sword above my head, I brought it down, aiming for the wolf's neck as all the hurt, the guilt, and the anger that had grown inside me since Cara had been taken rose to the surface, consuming me until all I saw was a monster and all I felt was justice.

"Raine, DON'T!" Kade roared behind me.

Seconds flew by as my sword came down, and my arm muscles screamed at the effort as I diverted my blade, bringing it down beside the wolf's head. Jarring pain shot up my arms as the sword connected with stone instead of soft wolf flesh.

The air burned as I sucked it into my lungs, staring at the wolf beneath me. But I didn't question Kade.

"Kasey!" howled one of the males behind me, but I didn't look to see who it was. Kasey had stopped moving. A dark pool of blood covered the floor around her wolf body, and her pale-gray eyes had closed.

I stared as I realized what I'd almost done. *But she'd tried to kill Kade.* I didn't feel guilty, but peering at the silent wolf made me feel colder somehow. Like something inside me had died.

Looking up, I turned my attention to the males. Kade's gaze connected with mine, and all I saw was sadness.

"You fucking bitch!" yelled a male with long brown hair that reached his shoulders. Fury raged in his green eyes. "I don't care if you're a newblood. I'll kill you for what you've done." Throwing his blade to the ground, he reached up to fist his shirt, tearing it from his body, and the other male beside him did the same.

"The Taratun will have our heads if you kill her!" Zacal shouted at his followers, but they weren't listening to their alpha.

Holy fucking shit. I watched in horror as their bodies shifted and re-formed until there were two wolves before me, snarling and snapping their jaws, saliva dripping onto the ground.

"RAINE!" Kade roared, lunging toward one of the wolves as the monsters shot forward at the same time. Kade's thick arms grabbed the closest wolf, wrapping around the silver wolf's furry neck in a vise grip as they both fell to the ground.

There was no point in running. I turned toward the black wolf who was barreling toward me. The wolf's sleek body jumped into the air, and I rolled to the side to avoid his gnashing jaws. Claws scratched against stone as the wolf skidded to a halt and rounded back toward me.

Springing to my feet, I took a step backward, only to find myself falling as my boot slipped on Kasey's blood. Pain ricocheted up my spine as my ass connected with the floor. I shuffled backward, my palms scratching against the ground.

The wolf lunged for me, a huge mass of sinewy muscle covered in black fur, and violence shone in his green eyes as he sought his revenge from me. Blood pounded in my ears. There was nothing around me I could use to save myself. The sword was too far out of my reach, and the wall of weapons was still too far away. *I'm going to die,* I thought as my body grew cold.

I wouldn't even get a chance to find Cara. To save her. I was a fool coming into this fight. I was a human in a world of monsters. I didn't have claws or fangs. But I couldn't bring myself to regret it. I'd fought. And that was all I'd tried to do since Cara had been taken. To find a way to make a difference rather than be a lamb that awaited the slaughter.

I'd *tried.* The wolf leaped into the air, jaws wide as he sailed toward me, and I braced for the impact. Braced for the pain as those fangs tore me to shreds.

The wolf's sharp claws reached toward me, each curved nail bringing the promise of death. His gaping mouth was inches from me, his breath hot and rancid on my face, when a massive brown wolf came from the side, smashing into him and sending him sprawling to the ground, away from me.

My fingers trembled as I blinked in surprise, still expecting the pain that didn't come. The huge brown wolf stood atop the black wolf, pinning the smaller wolf to the ground. The black wolf snarled from beneath the bigger wolf's paws, and the brown wolf let out a growl that shook the walls of the cavern and made my bones rattle.

The black wolf stopped struggling and went limp as he remained trapped under the stronger male. The brown wolf bent his head, puffing his breath onto the smaller wolf, and the black wolf seemed to shrink back, submitting to the stronger wolf.

Satisfied that the black wolf wasn't going to move, the brown wolf turned his golden gaze my way. *Kade.* I should have been shaken to my core at the sight of the wolf, but all I felt was relief. Fucking relief.

A clang sounded on the other side of the room, and the brown wolf's huge head turned to the noise. Zacal had knocked one of the axes as he moved along the shelf of weapons, backing toward the door. He froze as Kade's gaze bored into him.

The brown wolf growled in the face of the black wolf one more time before stalking toward where Zacal still remained in human form. Zacal's face was pale white, and even from here, I could see the rapid rise and fall of his chest as he stared at Kade's wolf.

The brown wolf prowled closer to him until he was only a couple yards from the male. Lifting his head, the wolf let out another growl that shook the walls, and Zacal cringed, his shoulders dipping down, his chest caving inward.

I stood and walked over to the sword that I'd used to stab Kasey. The black wolf's gaze watched me the entire time, but he remained where he was on the floor.

When I looked toward the brown wolf again, Kade was standing in his place, his wide shoulders squared, golden eyes blazing, and his head high.

"Take your wolves, Zacal, and get out of here before I decide to kill you," Kade growled, and even my pulse raced at his words. Gone was the male who was defeated, buried under his guilt. Here was a leader. An alpha.

Zacal lifted himself now that Kade was in human form, but he still pressed against the wall. "I'm the wolf alpha of the House of Worzen. You won't kill me. We both know you don't want to take my place. You're a traitor who left the wolves in your care to die. No one would follow you."

Kade paused, and I had no doubt the words still stung him. "Leave," he snarled again. "Tell no one of the newblood and what happened here. We both know if anyone hears of this, your time as alpha of the pack will come to a swift end." He peered over at the black wolf lying in submission on the floor. "How long do you think it will be until he starts questioning your leadership now that he's seen how weak you are?"

Zacal didn't answer, his lips forming a tight line.

Kade looked back again to the silver wolf, who lay unconscious on the floor, and the gray wolf, who still had blood leaking from her. "Get Kasey to a healer," he commanded, then he turned and strode toward me.

The muscles on Kade's naked body rippled with every step he took, and I forced myself to focus on his golden eyes. Gone were the shadows, and brightness sparked in the golden depths instead.

"Let's go," he said as he reached me and led me toward the door. Zacal's and the other male's eyes followed me as we strode from the room, but I didn't look at them. I was too preoccupied thinking about the male at my side.

CHAPTER 21

~ Raine ~

Kade only made it a few steps outside the door to the training cavern when he stumbled. I moved closer to him, draping one of his thick arms over my shoulders. The muscles of his arm tensed when I grabbed him, but he leaned onto me.

"You weigh a ton," I groused, lifting his arm higher when it started to slide off my shoulders, his skin slippery from all the blood. His head lowered as if it was taking all his effort not to collapse, but light still shone in his eyes, his golden gaze brighter than I'd ever seen it.

We staggered down the tunnel, and I peered over my shoulder to check Zacal and his wolves weren't following us. Turning forward again, I grunted at Kade's weight. "What the hell just happened?"

I hadn't expected him to answer, but to my surprise, he said, "I couldn't let them kill you."

I swallowed, not sure why hearing that made my stomach tighten. Then I remembered the bond and the fact the Taratun wanted me alive. How could I think he'd saved me for any other reason? "Because if I die, you die."

Kade didn't respond, and the tightening in my stomach was replaced by the pang of...something else. *Hurt?*

"Why didn't you fight the wolves when they first attacked you? You're obviously stronger. You could have ended it before it even began."

Kade still didn't answer, and even though the rational part of me knew he was bleeding out, it still pissed me off. I'd gone back for him. Risked my escape and my life for him. I knew I'd been foolish, but I didn't regret what I'd done. I tried not to think of the black wolf racing toward me, his gnashing jaws aiming for my head. It had been too close. If Kade hadn't turned...

"The least you can do is answer me after I went back for you," I said, my voice hard.

"You were reckless," Kade finally growled. "Zacal wouldn't have killed me. He just likes to prove his dominance in front of his wolves."

"Dominance? By beating up a wolf who isn't fighting back?"

"Something like that."

Confusion made my head hurt. "Why do you let him treat you like that?"

"If I force Zacal to submit, I'll have to take his place as alpha. The wolves respect strength. I don't deserve to be alpha of the House of Worzel."

"Really? Because it looked like he just submitted to you." I pictured Zacal with his shoulders tipped down and his back pressed against the wall of weapons. That male was no leader.

"Both of us need to be in wolf form for it to count. He knows my wolf would likely tear his apart. That's why he didn't shift. Today still won't look good for him, but the only other one watching was Roren, the black wolf. He's one of Zacal's most loyal followers. I doubt he'll say anything."

"From the looks of Zacal, the wolves would be better off with you as their alpha."

"They wouldn't," Kade said, his voice so cold goosebumps prickled up my arms. Pain had begun to creep back into his gaze, dimming the light in his eyes.

We walked in silence, and I wondered if he was reliving the moment that haunted his memories. If he was remembering whatever had happened with his family. His arm began sliding from my shoulders again, and I pulled it back behind my neck, ignoring the stickiness of his blood against my fingers. *Goddess*, there was so much blood. "Why aren't you healing like Asher?"

His golden gaze slid to me, and I saw the burning question there. *Did the horned monster not tell Kade about me stabbing him?* "All monsters heal faster than humans, but demons are the only ones who heal instantly. Wolves, like most monsters, can only be killed by having our heads severed from our bodies or being consumed in fire."

Something in my chest eased knowing that Kade would be all right. I tried to tell myself it was just the annoying magic that bonded us, but seeing Kade hurting for his family made me feel closer to him somehow. Like we were kindred spirits, both haunted by a past we couldn't change.

"Why did you make me save that gray wolf, Kasey?" I asked.

Kade sighed heavily. "She doesn't deserve to die. I failed them all. It wasn't just my family who was taken by the fae. I—" Kade cleared his throat, and I found myself aching for him. I could tell it was taking him a lot to speak about whatever had happened.

"I'd only been alpha for a month before the fae attacked," Kade continued. "I was out with Locke and the others on the opposite side of the city, celebrating, when a portal opened near the House of Worzel and the wolves were attacked. I heard the howls, but I couldn't get back fast enough. By the time I reached the house..." He paused, closing his eyes, and I could feel the tremble in his arm. Clenching his jaw, he opened his eyes, his gaze hard. "We lost twelve wolves that day."

Twelve. My stomach churned. Sure, I hated the monsters who took villagers from my island, but no one should have to lose their family. And I was starting to realize that not all the monsters in this world were the same. They were so much more like humans than I'd thought they'd be.

Before I could think, I moved closer to him, pulling his arm tighter around my neck, and brushing my side against his as I subconsciously tried to ease his pain. Warmth burned where our skin touched, the pull of our bond humming now that we were even closer.

Abruptly, Kade stopped walking, and he turned toward me, his head leaning down as his gaze bored into mine.

I knew I should pull away. I was too close to the monster. Within his grasp, without a weapon. His wolf was powerful, and so was he. But I didn't move.

"Thank you, Mahare," he growled softly.

Stunned, I stood staring at him before I recovered myself, my heart beating faster at the surprising tenderness with which he'd said the name. Swallowing, I said, "My name's Raine."

"I know," he said, his gaze not leaving mine. "Mahare means 'fiery one' in the ancient tongue."

I squirmed, feeling uncomfortable under his intense gaze. "Uh, don't mention it. Though, you were the one who saved my life."

For the first time since I'd met him, a small smile lifted his lips. "Why didn't you escape?"

I blinked in surprise. "How did you—?" And then it hit me. *He knew.* He knew I'd see the rocky shelf leading around the mountain, and that I'd try to escape. "If you knew I'd see a chance to escape, why send me up there?"

Kade started forward again, taking me with him. "I've never agreed with the trials. None of us do."

I didn't need to ask to know he was talking about Locke and the others. My brows slammed down. *What the actual hell?* Everything I thought I knew about these monsters was turned on its head, and my mind was left spinning, not sure what was truth and what was reality. "But if you don't agree, why were you guys the ones to take me and the other villagers from my island?"

"We have our reasons. This world is complicated."

I wanted to punch him for not answering my question, but I figured that would be a shitty thing to do considering his current state. After a moment of silence, I said, "I saw the reports and the invitation."

Kade's body tensed, and his steps slowed. "We've only played the part that we had to. Having newbloods every ten years helps to add fresh blood to the houses and some use it as an opportunity to find mates. We're immortal. You'd be surprised how the Week of Orash increases morale. A large portion of Katakin shows up to watch the fights, including the alphas from each of the houses."

My anger from earlier, when I'd found the papers, rose back to the surface. Even if he didn't agree with what was happening to us humans, he was still a part of it. "Mates? So you let them use us?"

A growl rumbled from Kade's chest. "It's not like that. The humans change when they become monsters. Most of them want to be chosen by the higher houses. I've heard some are even grateful they were taken from your island. They're treated like goddesses by the members of the house, given everything they could possibly want. And they don't have to accept a mate if they don't want to."

"Grateful?" I scoffed, struggling to process what I was hearing. But then I imagined Lana. From everything I'd learned, the reason she hadn't emerged from the black water when we'd first arrived here wasn't because she'd died. It was because she'd *changed*. I could imagine her thriving while she was doted upon, treated like royalty. "And what about the ones who don't want to join a house?" I asked, my voice quieter as I thought of my sweet sister, Cara.

"All newbloods must join a house," Kade admitted. "But they have a say in which house they go with. The Week of Orash is a time for the newbloods to showcase their new skills and also for members of the houses to assess who might be a good fit for them. Every newblood has the right to refuse an offer from any house. If a newblood is presented with an offer from their respective high house but they don't want to accept it, they can choose one of the respective lower houses. The newbloods always find their place."

I frowned, but the tension that had been pulling at me eased. Cara hadn't chosen to come here, but at least she'd had a choice with what house she went to live with. I still had no clue where she was, but this knowledge helped ease my worries. "Are you, Locke, and the others from your respective high houses?"

Kade's eyes darkened. "We're not a part of any house. Not anymore. I'm sure you'll find a house that suits you."

It was then that I realized he thought I was worried about where I was going to end up. I didn't care about that. I had no intention of joining any house. I just wanted to find Cara.

"Break the bond between us and bond to the members of the house you choose. If you find a mate, bond to them instead. I can't protect you."

I glared at him. "Like I said, I didn't bond to you. I don't know what this is between us. And you don't have to worry. I can take care of myself."

His voice was quiet, but his eyes glowed brighter as we staggered along. "That you can, Mahare."

CHAPTER 22

~ Kade ~

I stared into Raine's amber eyes, the color only a shade darker than my own, with small flecks of red mixing with the orange, like fires burned within them. *Mahare.* That was what I'd called her. A fitting name for the human who was starting to burn her way through my defenses.

She was strong, willful, and loyal... *To me?* I'd done nothing to deserve her loyalty. With how she'd been treated since coming here, I hadn't been surprised to wake up finding her about to stab me with that letter opener.

I knew the role I played in bringing her here, away from that island. But she'd come back for me. Had tried to *protect* me against Zacal. A human, standing up to monsters. This female was fierce, even without monster abilities.

Since that dark night my family and the other wolves had been slaughtered, I'd let Zacal take over the pack, and he'd used every opportunity to beat me down in front of the other wolves.

They knew I was stronger, but when Zacal constantly forced me to submit, it was easier for them to accept him as their leader. It wouldn't have taken much for me to put him back in his place and to reclaim what had been mine, but I never did. I welcomed the pain he inflicted on me. I'd failed the wolves, and I deserved the punishment.

But today had been different because *she* had been there. The outrageously beautiful human with the sassy mouth. The human who'd tried to kill me while I'd slept. It wasn't just the bond that was between us, the magic that urged me to protect her. There was a fire in her that reminded me of who I used to be. Reminded me of a life that had once been mine. I couldn't let them kill her.

I hadn't even been thinking about the bond and the fact that her death would have meant my own and those of my brothers. I saw those wide amber eyes staring at Roren, still fierce even when staring at the face of death, and I'd instantly relinquished control, letting my wolf take over our body. She'd needed him, and I wouldn't let her be torn apart.

My wolf had been all too happy to join the fray. I'd forced his dominance down for so long that our blood had sung as I'd released him. And now, with Raine's skin burning against mine, I could feel him just under the surface. Sated by the action in the training cavern but desperate to be with her. To claim her. Protect her. He didn't care if she turned into a wolf shifter or not.

We couldn't have her, and my wolf roared at the thought of her choosing to be with another, but for now, we'd do our best to protect her like the bond wanted us to. We couldn't save our family, but we could protect her until she chose a house.

My mouth dried out at the thought of the little human going to live with one of the houses. My arm threatened to slide from her shoulders, but her hand held me firmly, her body keeping me upright. My gaze slid to where her breasts were almost popping out of Lyr's outfit, and her dry chuckle met my ears.

"Eyes are up here," she said with a smirk, and I moved my gaze back to her face. Blood was splattered over her tan skin, and sweat had plastered her red hair to her forehead.

"Drink the pink liquid," I said, remembering that I hadn't seen her drink much since she'd come to our room.

"I'm more of a plain water kind of girl," she responded coolly.

If I was going to protect her, I figured I'd better start. "You need to drink it."

"Last time someone told me to drink something, I ended up with blood in my mouth. Thanks, but no thanks."

"It's for your safety," I persisted. "It's given to all the humans when they arrive and the newbloods."

"Safety? And here I thought you were poisoning me," she said while regarding me.

"It contains Acaralia, a native herb that will prevent a babe from growing in your belly."

She stopped abruptly, her eyes flaring wide. "Wait...it's *birth control*?" Her mouth dropped open, and the expression was almost comical.

My face remained passive, and I shrugged, not understanding her reaction. "If a human becomes pregnant before they turn, when they transform into a monster either the babe is killed as she changes, or the mother is torn apart when the babe turns. It's also well-known that newbloods have high libidos. Until they join a house, they're free to bed whomever they want. The Acaralia prevents the creation of crossbreeds."

"Good thing I don't plan on sleeping with any of you assholes."

I raised a thick brow, remembering how I'd woken up between her thighs, even if she had been planning to kill me. If the bond had any of the same effects on her as it did on me, it was a wonder she hadn't already bedded one of us. Just thinking about it was making my cock hard. But that was not why I was telling her this.

"Like I said, there are worse monsters out there than us," I growled. I hoped she got my meaning after meeting Zacal. "And we're telling monsters that you've already turned. No one will think you're human."

I could see her mind working. Her brow crinkled as she processed my words. Eventually, she nodded, and we began walking again. "This world just keeps getting better and better," she muttered.

I didn't answer, and I didn't think she expected me to. My head was light with the loss of blood, and it was a wonder I was even managing to stand.

· · · · ● · ● · · · ·

~ Locke ~

I scented Kade's blood on the air and raced up the tunnel. *Fucking Halced, finally.* Darian and Asher followed behind me, keeping up easily. The three of us had been searching the mountain since we'd all woken from sleep, a blinding pain in our chests. We'd bolted out of bed, but by the time the three of us were in the tunnels, the pain had disappeared, the bond between us and Raine calming, so we had no idea where the human was.

Rounding the bend of the tunnel, a long breath escaped me when I spotted them up ahead. Two heads lifted as we approached, amber and blazing golden eyes peering at me. I didn't pause to think about how Kade's eyes were glowing brighter than they had in over a century.

Stopping in front of them, my gaze swept over where Raine stood, Kade's arm hooked over her shoulders. Black blood splattered over her, and my nostrils flared as I breathed in deeper, checking for any scent of her blood. Satisfied when I didn't notice anything unusual, I turned to my wolf brother. He was smeared with black, his naked body brutalized with wounds, and I had an idea who had given him the treatment.

My shoulders became rigid, and my eye twitched. "What happened?"

"Went to the training room," Kade said in a low voice. "Zacal and a few of his wolves showed up."

My lips pressed together into a thin line as I tried to contain my anger. If Kade only let me fight the pathetic wolf alpha, Zacal, we wouldn't have been dealing with this shit. I wouldn't kill the wolf. That would bring the council down on us, but I could have taught him a lesson. Kade didn't deserve the treatment Zacal and his followers were all too happy to give him.

"Fucking hell," Asher breathed behind me.

My fury only grew when I thought of the fact Raine had been there. Zacal should have known better than to mess with a newblood, but I didn't trust the slimy bastard. Had he touched her? *Fuck.*

I shouldn't have cared. I *didn't* fucking care. Or that was what I told myself. There was no pain in my chest, so if we were right about the bond, that meant Raine wasn't in danger. My attention went back to her, but from the fire that burned in her eyes, I knew she was unharmed.

"Where the fuck are they, Kade?" I asked, my voice lethal.

Asher moved forward, taking the burden of Kade from Raine and draping Kade's arm over his own shoulders. Darian grabbed Kade's other arm.

"We took care of it," Kade said, and his lip tipped upward into a half grimace, half smile.

We? I didn't get the chance to ask what he meant.

"What the fuck, Kade? Are you smilin'? I didn' even know your lips could still do that," Asher said.

Darian laughed. "And here I thought the human might try to slit your throat while you slept. From the looks of it, she saved you."

Asher and Darian walked with Kade down the tunnel, and I moved into step beside Raine who was following behind them. Her gaze was fixed on the deep wounds that had been carved into Kade's back. They were bad, but nothing he wouldn't heal from.

As we walked, I was shocked to find my anger dissolved as I stared at Raine. I took in her sweat-slick body, and couldn't stop looking at where her thick, wavy hair curled down to the small of her back.

"He's been like that since his family passed, hasn't he?" she said, her voice quiet.

My mouth refused to work as I wondered exactly what had gone down with Zacal and the wolves. From the pair of them, it was obvious they'd fought. Had *Kade* finally fought back?

"Yes," I said, not wanting to give anything else away. It was Kade's story to tell, if he hadn't already.

She simply nodded as if all I'd done was confirm her own thoughts.

"What happened, Raine?" I asked.

She blinked up at me as if she was surprised I had used her name. I couldn't blame her, because I felt the same way. It had just slipped out, the sound of it feeling so delicious and right on my tongue. Like she was a part of our group and always had been.

I shut down my emotions, my expression becoming hard. She wasn't a part of our group. We couldn't claim her.

Confusion crossed her face as she watched me, but she said, "Zacal gave me a valuable lesson about this world."

My nostrils flared, a trace of something that couldn't possibly be fear working into my thoughts as I again wondered if Zacal had laid a hand on her. I sniffed again, but I couldn't detect any trace of him on her, or any of the other wolves. "And what lesson was that, beautiful?" I asked.

She swallowed, and I watched the slight bobbing of her neck, noting the veins that rested just beneath her skin. "That you're not the bad guys."

Caught off guard, I opened my mouth to correct her. We'd done plenty of bad shit in our time, usually to appease my father, but I closed my mouth again without saying anything. If she wanted to pretend we were the good guys, I'd let her. Maybe it'd make her less likely to try to escape. And, deep down, there was a part of me that wished she was right.

CHAPTER 23

~ Raine ~

Kade passed out not long after the others had found us, but we made it back to their rooms quicker once Asher hefted Kade over his shoulder and carried him the rest of the way. Asher placed Kade onto a settee, and I watched as Locke grabbed a medical kit and Darian cleaned Kade's wounds, smearing a blue ointment on each one.

Darian's fingers were swift as they worked on Kade's body, tending to him, and I had a feeling he was the main healer of the group. The three of them were an efficient team, and I had to force myself not to think about how many other times Kade had let Zacal and his followers leave him in a similar state.

I thought of all that Kade had told me on our walk back after dealing with those wolves. What the hell was I doing? I'd risked my escape, nearly gotten myself killed, and still had no idea where Cara was. From what Kade had said, Cara had been given the choice of which house she belonged to, so there was that, at least. Still, how was I supposed to find her in a world of monsters? I didn't even know what kind of monster she'd turned into.

I'd been so desperate to escape before, but after seeing what Zacal and his fellow wolves were like, I was starting to wonder whether Kade was right. What would happen if one of the other monsters out there captured me? At least I knew these monsters wouldn't kill me. This bond stopped them from doing so, and they didn't want to anger the Taratun.

I didn't really worry about death, but if I was dead, I couldn't find Cara. For the first time since coming here, I wished I would turn into a damn monster already. If I was a monster it'd be easier for me to find her as my new abilities would make me stronger, faster, and quicker to heal. *Demon. You should turn into a demon.* I thought of the way Asher healed, his skin knitting together after he pulled my dagger from his flesh. That would be damn handy. I didn't care that it'd mean I'd have horns and a tail.

Sighing, I left the others tending to Kade and used the washroom. After relieving myself and washing my face, I went back to the common room and gulped from the jug of pink liquid on the table to ease my dry throat.

They'd placed Kade on his bed, and I went to check on him. The male was still stark naked, and I moved closer to him, inspecting his wounds. My eyes widened when

I noticed they had already grown smaller. *Holy Goddess.* Whatever the blue ointment was that they'd smeared over him, it was working. *Definitely need to turn into a monster.*

"Let's go, beautiful," Locke said as he watched me. "You can stay in my room for the rest of the day."

A strange surge of excitement went through me at the idea of seeing Locke's bedroom, but I shook my head. "I'm sleeping here."

Curiosity shone in Locke's black eyes, but he didn't speak as he left me alone with Kade and closed the door. I knew he was probably waiting in the common room, making sure that I didn't sneak out of Kade's room while the male was unconscious and escape, but I didn't care.

Moving back, I stared at the other side of the bed. Exhaustion dragged at me, and the leather outfit I wore had begun to chafe. I was grateful for Lyr's clothing, really, but the ladies were definitely *not* a fan.

Peering at the wardrobe, I opened it to find Kade's clothes neatly arranged inside. Plucking out one of his huge shirts, I wiggled out of the leather outfit, rubbed the red marks on my breasts, and slid the shirt over my head. *I'll change back as soon as I wake.* I knew it wasn't the best idea, but Kade wasn't going to be up anytime soon.

The blanket was pinned under Kade's large form, and my gaze slid to the floor, then back to the bed. There was no way I was prying it out from under him. *If I stay on the other side of the bed, we'll never be touching.* Carefully, I lay on the edge of the mattress, turned my back to the male on the other side, and closed my eyes.

· · · ●·●·· ·

I sat up suddenly and squinted in the dim light. Kade was no longer lying on the other side of the bed, the empty space illuminated by the blue hue of a single lit torch near the door. The darkness seemed to swell around me, clinging to the edges of the mattress, and my hand dropped to my thigh before I remembered my dagger wasn't there.

Movement in the corner of the room caught my eye, and I turned to see Locke step from the shadows. His wings and claws were nowhere to be seen, but his predatory gaze was so dark it sent a shiver down my spine.

Faster than I thought possible, he moved closer, appearing beside me. He stretched out on the bed and propped himself up with one arm. What the—? *Where his shirt had been was now a pale, sculpted chest, and his muscles shone in the blue light when he moved to lean toward me.* "I told you I'd enjoy devouring you, beautiful," *he said in my ear, his voice a low rasp. His lips trailed down my shoulder, the soft tips of his fangs lightly scraping against my skin, and I shuddered.*

I tried to lift my hands to push him away from me, only to find my wrists were now tied above my head, the rope tight against my skin. Kade's shirt was no longer on me, and my exposed nipples puckered in the cool air.

Opening my mouth, I tried to curse at Locke, but no words came out. He smirked down at me, his fangs peeking between the curve of his sinful lips.

I should have fought him. My legs were free, and I should have twisted my body to kick at him, but... I wasn't afraid. The bond between us hummed at his proximity, making my body tingle. Goddess, I wanted him.

Kade appeared from the darkness on the other side of me, his broad form taking a similar stance to Locke's, his naked body lying on the bed, not a single wound on him. He leaned down to kiss the soft hollow of my neck, chased up by a kiss to my jaw, then his teeth clamped onto my earlobe. "Do you want this, Mahare?" he growled, and I squirmed as need made my core clench.

"I—" My words turned to a gasp as Locke's cool hand splayed across my belly and his mouth found my breast, his tongue flicking at my nipple. Pleasure rushed through my body as he sucked and licked, his hand sliding up from my belly to palm my other breast.

Kade's hot breath puffed in my ear as his fingers slid between my legs, teasing my wetness. I writhed on the mattress, wanting more. Needing *more.*

Needing *them.*

Violet and crystal-blue eyes glowed in the darkness near the wall, and excitement wound through me at the thought that Asher and Darian were watching us.

A moan squeezed from between my lips as Kade's fingers glided into me, and Locke's teeth sunk into the skin above my breast...

• • • • • • • • • •

My eyes sprang open, and I sucked in a huge, gasping breath, my lungs starved as if my body had momentarily forgotten it needed air. Sweat slipped down my temples, and I shifted my legs, feeling the dampness between my thighs.

A dream. It was just a dream. I said the words in my mind like a mantra as I tried to remind myself of my reality and calm my racing heartbeat. *Monsters. They're monsters. Seriously, what is wrong with me?* It was official. I'd lost my mind, and I wasn't sure if I'd ever regain my sanity. Even now, desire left my body aching with need.

"You talk in your sleep, Mahare," said a deep voice beside me, and I jolted as I turned to find Kade's body next to mine.

"What the hell?" I said, jerking my head back. "Ever heard of staying on your side of the bed?"

Amusement shone in his golden eyes. They were bright again, like they had been after he'd shifted to wolf form when we'd fought Zacal and the other wolves. "I am on my side," he growled.

Frowning, I tore my gaze from his to peer behind me. Sure enough, a long section of bed lay bare behind me. I was the one who had moved right next to Kade, as if I'd tried to get closer to him while I was sleeping. *Traitorous body.*

"How are you feeling?" I blurted, wanting to distract him from the fact I couldn't even control myself while I slept.

Kade stretched his limbs. "*Much* better."

I scanned his face. The gash that had crossed his cheek was completely gone, and only the faint trace of blue remained. My gaze then lowered to see his muscled chest and arms were healed as well. I didn't need to look any lower to know the rest of his body was the same. *Being a monster has some serious perks.*

Lifting my hand, I went to touch where a wound had previously been across his bare chest, but realizing what I was doing, I stopped myself. My cheeks flushed, and I started to pull my hand away, but Kade gripped my wrist. I could have yanked my hand back if I'd wanted, but I stilled, waiting to see what he would do.

"What were you dreaming about?" he asked. His golden gaze burned into me, and my pulse raced at the lust banked in his eyes.

I remembered Locke's teeth sinking into the flesh above my breast while Kade's fingers filled me, torturously slow, and I swallowed thickly. *What did I say in my sleep? Fuck, did I moan?* "Nothing," I lied.

"It was most definitely not nothing," Kade said, his nostrils flaring as he scented the air.

Damn wolf senses. "I was just thinking about how much I hate you assholes," I said, but my husky breath betrayed my lie.

His answering grin made my stomach flip. This was the second time I'd seen him smile since the fight with Zacal and his wolves, and I couldn't deny the effect seeing him smile had on me. To know I'd helped put it there. Something had changed between us since the fight, and something had changed in *him*. The bond between us was already hard to resist, but I was starting to realize that there was a part of me that didn't *want* to resist it.

I'd been on my own for so damn long that the idea of being *close* to someone again was alluring. I wasn't a virgin. I'd been with a boy called Raylen back on the island. We'd fooled around years ago, but when he had found out I planned to purposely get chosen by the monsters, he'd been quick to move on.

Smart guy. It didn't really bother me. I couldn't afford to get attached to anyone anyway. It wasn't fair to them, or me. But now—now I wondered if I could have it. Just this once. I would still find Cara. I had to. But would it hurt if I let my guard down this one time?

"I don't believe you." Kade's voice rumbled in my ear. He pressed a soft kiss to my collarbone, and I closed my eyes, feeling my heart thudding in my chest.

I went to press my thighs together, but his hand slid up the shirt I was wearing and between my legs, pushing them apart. *Fuck. I shouldn't.* He was a monster, but... I was going to turn into a monster as well anyway, wasn't I? If what he'd said was true, he hated the part he played in the trials. And from what I'd seen, he was like me. Buried by the guilt of the past.

Just once. Maybe just this one time we could both have some fun. Kade's fingers hooked into my panties and pulled, ripping them from me. He flung them to the side of the bed, and then his fingers were sliding against my clit, massaging and sending pleasure spiraling through me as if we were picking up right where we'd left off in my dream.

Holy Mother Falia. It had never felt like this with Raylen. Sure, it had felt good, but all I had was Kade's fingers and my release was already rising, my body coiled with pleasure.

"Tell me the truth, Mahare. Were you dreaming about me?" Kade coaxed, desire making his voice even deeper.

I ground my teeth in defiance, determined to show I was still in control, but he slipped two fingers into me, and I realized I didn't give a fuck whether he knew or not. He pulled his fingers slowly back out and teased my entrance. "Yes," I gasped, desperate to feel him inside me again.

A low growl rumbled in his throat, and he rewarded me by sliding his fingers back in, pumping them in and out of my body. He grazed his teeth against the soft skin of my shoulder, but he didn't bite. His shoulders shook, as if from the effort of keeping himself restrained.

I tried to clench around his fingers, but he chuckled, pulling them back out and sliding them up the length of me again, lingering every so often to massage my clit. "Was I the only one?" His voice was guttural, and the sound melted my insides.

I wiggled on the bed, trying to encourage him to move his fingers back inside me, but he just stared at me with those intense golden eyes. The gold flared brighter as he watched me, and his ears started to form points, but he shook his head, and the color dulled slightly, his ears becoming round again.

His fingers trailed down from my clit, only the tips sliding inside me, and I knew what he was waiting for. *Asshole.* "No," I finally admitted. "Locke and the others were there, too." My chest rose and fell as I watched him carefully, not sure how he'd react.

The hunger in his gaze intensified, his eyes narrowing, but his only response was to push the full length of his fingers into me and begin pumping them in and out, increasing his speed all while watching me intently.

Oh, Goddess. I moaned, unable to stop myself as his other hand slid under the shirt and his callused fingers brushed over my peaked nipple. He slowed, moving lower on the bed as his free hand lifted my shirt higher. I swallowed in anticipation, and the moment his tongue began licking my clit, his fingers sliding in and out of me, stars burst before my eyes, and I tipped over the edge, my hands gripping the blanket beneath me as I came undone.

When I stopped trembling, he prowled on top of me, his breathing as ragged as mine. Leaning down, he ground his hard body against me, letting me feel every taught muscle and the considerable hardness between his legs.

"We should stop," he said. *Thank the Goddess he has some sense.* I sure as hell didn't. I'd had a taste, and I wanted *more.*

Kade kept speaking. "My wolf wants me to claim you. To leave my mark and my scent all over you so every fucking monster knows you belong to us."

Well, damn. I'd never heard of claiming until coming here, but the idea of being Kade's sent a confusing thrill through me.

"But we can't claim you," Kade growled, frustrated, his head lowering as he nipped his teeth lightly against my neck. "We don't know what monster you're becoming yet, and you'll have to compete during the Week of Orash." His voice grew quieter. "When you turn, you'll have offers from many monsters. There's no way they won't want you."

Won't be a problem. I have no intention of belonging to a house, let alone a monster. "You're right," I agreed weakly. "We should stop."

Kade remained above me, and my breath hitched as I stared up at him. His russet-colored hair was mussed from sleep, and I couldn't help admiring how ruggedly beautiful he was, even with the bed hair. And how he looked so...*human.*

Without thinking, I leaned forward, pressing my lips against his. The bond between us sparked, warming my body as he kissed me back, his lips all too eager to meet mine. Our kiss was like fire, burning through me, consuming me until I was thinking of nothing else.

He pushed my head back onto the pillow as his tongue slipped into my mouth, the kiss becoming more desperate. The growl that left him vibrated against my lips, my tongue.

He moved his body, his cock pressing against the soft skin under my belly, and I lifted my left thigh, letting him slide along my wetness, the sensation making my body shudder.

When he didn't give me what I wanted, I pulled away from his kiss. "Stop teasing," I hissed, my own frustration growing. I needed this. For one night, I could have this. I could block out this fucked-up world I was in. I could forget about my guilt and just have this one thing. This one very *large* thing. I wasn't even sure if it would fit inside me, but I wanted to try.

His chuckle was dark but strained.

I ground against him, and the tip of his cock slid inside me. "Fucking hell," he growled. "If we do this, you can't let me bite you. You can't let me claim you. Even if you have to fight me off to stop me."

"Not a problem," I said, my voice breathy. "Fighting assholes is a specialty of mine."

His golden eyes narrowed, and his lips twitched upward. "That it is, Mahare."

I gasped as he slid into me, his hardness stretching and filling me, driving so deliciously deep. My fingers dug into his muscular shoulders, and the growl that left his throat was carnal and wild. Possessive.

His shoulders shook, and his face tightened with strain, as if he was trying to keep the wolf contained within him. Pointed fangs peeked from between his lips. *Ho-ly fuck.* I realized he wasn't joking when he'd said I might have to fight him. There was a war within him, between him and his beast, and I was going to have to knock the fucker out.

He pulled his cock out and slammed it in again, touching parts so deep inside me that it took the air from my lungs. I moaned, my back arching off the bed. I wanted this. I *needed* this. He was just going to have to control himself.

When he slid out of me again, I pushed against his right shoulder. Understanding what I was doing, he moved with me. In a smooth motion, he flipped, his back landing on the bed and my thighs reaching over to straddle him.

I pulled his shirt from me, tossing it to the floor, and glided onto him. A small cry of pleasure left me as he filled me again, my eyes closing and my head tipping back. He lifted his hands, cupping my breasts, and I whimpered at the touch.

Opening my eyes, I rode him hard and fast, my pleasure building as he slid in and out of me over and over until my thighs burned from the effort and sweat slid down the curve of my back.

He lifted his chest off the bed, his eyes bright gold and his fangs bared as a growl so loud it made the bed shake ripped from his throat. His gaze fixed on the soft skin of my right shoulder, but I pushed him back down, my palms against his chest. "Not today, Wolfie," I said, staring him in the eye.

His skin was hot under my fingers, and I knew he could overpower me if he wanted, but he settled his head back against the pillow, accepting my command. His golden gaze watched me through hooded eyes as I drove us closer to our release.

He lifted his hips slightly, driving himself deeper again, and it all became too much. Light exploded behind my eyes as pleasure erupted in my body, the feeling so intense, so freeing, that I gasped, overwhelmed by the flood of sensation. Tingles swept through my body as Kade spilled his own release into me, and I felt as though I was floating. Like for the first time, the weight of the last ten years had been lifted from my shoulders, and all that was left was the pleasure.

As the feeling subsided, exhaustion pulled at me, and I slumped onto Kade's heaving chest, my own breathing still rapid, my heartbeat loud in my ears.

"You will be the death of me, Mahare," Kade said softly in my ear and kissed my temple. I peered up at him to see his eyes were blazing gold in the dim light.

He wasn't wrong. I thought of how the last time we'd been in his bed, I had tried to stab him. But then I thought of Cara. Of the invitation I'd found in his drawer only a few steps away, and my expression sobered.

He frowned as he watched me. "What is it?"

I hated to ruin whatever moment we were having, but I had to. I rolled off him onto the mattress. *It was just sex. Damn good sex, but still just sex. It can't be anything else.* Steeling myself, I said, "Ten years ago. What happened to the villagers who were taken?"

Kade's lips formed a thin line. "Same as the time before," he said. "They turned into monsters and joined houses, became part of our world, our society."

My heart began racing again as I realized this was the first time I might actually get the answer to the question that haunted me. My whole reason for going there. "A girl was chosen who was only sixteen at the time. She has mousy brown hair and wide brown eyes. Do you know what happened to her? Her name's Cara."

Kade didn't answer straightaway, and I held my breath.

"We weren't in charge of selecting the last round of humans or putting them through the trials," he finally said, and I released the breath I was holding as disappointment washed over me.

"But I watched all the fights during the Week of Orash," he continued. "The newbloods all joined houses, and most of them found mates. I don't know of anyone who went by the name Cara."

My shoulders sagged, and my mind went to the night Cara had been taken. Had she given the monsters a different name, or was it possible she hadn't competed in the Week of Orash?

"Who is she to you?" Kade asked.

I swallowed the lump that had grown in my throat. "A friend."

"Are you sure your friend was selected?" Kade said, his gravelly voice soft as if he had some understanding of what Cara meant to me.

My mind whirled. The image of Cara being led into the mouth of Procus was burned into my mind. She'd walked through the portal. I just had to find out where exactly she'd gone.

Kade lifted his arm and shifted closer to me, tucking me against him, and I didn't fight it. My eyes had grown heavy, and for the first time in years, I let myself fall asleep with a warm body by my side.

CHAPTER 24

~ Locke ~

I watched Kade, who was busy sharpening one of his swords, his muscled arms sliding the long blade back and forth along a whetstone. When night had come he'd exited his room, used the washroom, and without even acknowledging Asher, Darian, and me, had set about sharpening his sword.

Raine had entered the washroom after him, wearing nothing but Kade's shirt and with her leather outfit tucked under her arm.

Kade knew we'd smelled her on him. Before he'd entered the washroom, her scent had clung to him in a way that could only mean one thing. Not that we didn't already know by the moans that had come from his room. Moans that'd had my pants tightening uncomfortably while I'd tried reading the book that was propped on my lap.

"Well, I, for one, think we need to revisit whose room our lovely Raine sleeps in during the day," Darian drawled, sipping from a goblet of wine even though the night had only just begun.

"I second that," Asher added with a mischievous grin.

I watched my wolf brother curiously, noting the way his eyes glowed brighter than I'd seen them in decades, and his lips twitched up slightly in a half smile. That was right, *a fucking smile*. I was glad he was happy. Kade had beaten himself up about his family for too damn long. Shadows still clung to his eyes, but it was there. The spark of something else. Something other than guilt. The wolf shifter I used to know was rising back to the surface. Maybe not entirely, but it was there. Still, I couldn't explain the annoyance that had my jaw clenching as I thought of him with Raine.

"You can't claim her," I reminded him, my voice cold. "None of us can." We didn't know what monster she would become. Mates had to be of the same breed. Not to mention we didn't belong to a house. Not that she'd want us to claim her. We had nothing to offer. We were broken. Shunned. We were powerful alphas who had run from the duties we had to our houses. It didn't matter if we all had our reasons. All that mattered in this fucking place was power and those who wielded it.

"I'm not an imbecile," Kade growled.

"Could have fooled me," I replied, my voice devoid of emotion.

The four of us were silent for a long while, brooding, with the crackle of the fire and the scrape of Kade's blade gliding against stone the only sounds.

Finally, Asher sighed and spoke. "I still can't believe she hasn' changed."

Lifting from my spot, I strode over to grab a drink. Darian had the right idea.

I'd just finished filling my goblet when Raine stepped out of the washroom, her hair damp and one of Lyr's ludicrously sexy outfits hugging her body, her breasts practically falling out of the leather. *Fucking Enzal*, the female was tempting as fuck. And Kade had been all over her.

There were no rules against fucking the newbloods or humans. It didn't matter who they were with as long as they were drinking the pink water with Acaralia in it to make sure a babe didn't grow in their bellies, and as long as no one tried to claim them. Monsters could only claim a newblood as a mate after the newblood had joined a house and if they were of the same breed. Still, I hadn't thought Kade would be the one to bed a human. Darian and Asher I expected, but not Kade. After the incident with his family, I could count on one hand the number of females he'd been with.

Raine's gaze was hard as she strolled right to the table laden with fresh fruits and sliced meat and began pulling fruit onto a plate. Then, without a word, she went over and dropped down onto the settee closest to Kade and began picking at her food.

I narrowed my eyes, watching as she wiggled, getting more comfortable. She wasn't sitting in just any spot. She was in *my* spot. *Definitely has a death wish.* The thought made my lips twitch.

As though she'd heard my thought, she lifted her head and returned my stare, challenge shining in her eyes. Like she was daring me to question her seating choice. This fucking human had balls. I had to give her that.

"If you want to see what a real monster's like, come join me, Sharachi," Asher said, pulling her attention away from me. He winked at Raine as he made his way to the washroom.

Darian rolled his eyes. "Ignore him, Raine lovely. We haven't visited the city in weeks, and Ash isn't used to his cock being so dry."

Raine choked on her mouthful, and I couldn't help my smirk as I watched her splutter, her cheeks reddening. It was adorable. Innocent. Delicious.

"Good to know," she finally managed, peering at Darian. Twisting her head, her gaze flitted to the washroom door and then back to the siren. "Why does he keep calling me Sharachi?"

"Ah," Darian responded with a sensual smile. He leaned forward, resting an elbow on his thigh and stroking his chin. "Sharachi is the name of one of the seven devils of the underworld. The female devil of seduction and war, who toys with males to bring them to their knees, causing chaos wherever she goes."

Raine's mouth dropped open. "He named me after one of the devils you believe in?" she said incredulously.

Darian shrugged. "We used to believe in six gods and goddesses as well, but belief in them died out soon after the curse. Think of it as a compliment." He leaned back on the settee, folding one leg over the other and studied her and Kade. "So are you both going to tell us what truly happened with Zacal?" he asked.

"There's nothing else to tell," Kade said, still sharpening his sword, though I didn't miss the slight shifting of his body, as if he was subconsciously trying to move closer to Raine. "I doubt he'll bother us for a while."

Something about Kade's last words had my sharp gaze fixing on Raine's face. I was still struggling to believe there was a human sitting here in our rooms, let alone one that had helped Kade fight Zacal and his wolves.

And just the night before, she'd refused to sit, but here she was, relaxed as if she belonged. *With us.* I tried to bury the thought. I didn't need to take in another stray. Not that she was like that. I wasn't fool enough to think Kade's cock had made her actually *like* us monsters. No, she had a goal. I could see it in her eyes. She was just biding her time until she got what she wanted, and I was itching to find out what it was.

She'd be formidable during the Week of Orash. When she turned, there was no way the members of her respective high house wouldn't want her, and then of course there were all those from the lower houses. I also didn't doubt monsters would be lining up to fight for the right to claim her as a mate.

No, my brothers and I couldn't offer her anything good in this world. All we had to give were tortured souls and our enemies. She'd already had to deal with Zacal.

But until she'd turned into a monster and joined a house, she was vulnerable. We had to find a way to get her to change. If we didn't, her life was in danger. And so was ours.

I was going to continue enjoying testing the human until she turned. I loved playing with pretty things.

· · · ● ·● · · ·

~ Raine ~

I shouldn't have been with Kade. Now that my mind was clearer, I knew I'd made a mistake. Sex just made things complicated. Messy. And I had to find Cara.

But even now, I wanted him. *Craved* him. I wanted more. My mind flitted to the dream I'd had with Locke and the others. For years, I'd gone without, but now I wanted them. *All* of them. I'd thought being with Kade might have eased my need, but it had only made it worse. Like I was a bear who'd had a taste of honey, but I wanted the whole hive.

No one had multiple partners back on the island. But staring at these males, these monsters, my bond pulled me toward all of them. Kade hadn't been angry when I'd admitted I'd been dreaming about the others as well. And knowing that...excited me.

Fuck, I was messed up. But for now, I was here. My best chance of finding Cara was to participate in the Week of Orash. I'd pretend to be a shifter and fight the other newbloods. If what Kade had said was right, all the alphas from each of the houses would be there, along with hordes of other monsters. If anyone knew what had happened to Cara, they would be there. If I was super lucky, Cara herself might even be there.

So I'd play their games. And if I got to enjoy Kade while I was at it, I wasn't going to complain.

I shifted further back on the settee and sighed contentedly, enjoying the tick of irritation on Locke's face. I hadn't intended to sit in his spot. It was only after I'd sat down and taken in his murderous glare that I'd realized. But like hell was I going to move.

His heated gaze slid over me, watching me, and my body warmed in response. Out of the four, Locke was the most dangerous. Those dark eyes were always paying attention, taking in everything around him.

I set down my now empty plate and filled a goblet with pink water from the jug on the table in front of me. Smiling, I downed the whole goblet, and I could have sworn Locke's eyes darkened further. If such a thing was possible. Was he aware I knew the truth of why I needed to drink it?

Something rumbled in Kade's chest where he stood close to me. *Goddess*, what was I doing?

I'd just set down the goblet, when Locke's gaze shot to the room's door, and he moved faster than I thought possible, stopping to stand in front of me. As if his movement was a signal, Kade copied his stance, moving beside Locke, and Darian stood, his back straight and muscles tensing as he glared at the door. *What the hell?*

The door opened, and I peered around Locke's legs to see a tall male stroll into the room. The male looked only a few years older than Locke and the others, perhaps mid-thirties, with a long button up coat covering his lean frame. His raven-colored hair was sleeked back from his gaunt face, and his eyes were black like Locke's, but they were colder, lifeless.

The newcomer's gaze locked on me, and my pulse quickened as a smile stretched across his face, his pale lips widening. There was something in the way he looked at me that made me feel like he'd been searching for me, and he was delighted he'd found his next victim. I stood, stepping around to Kade's side.

Every instinct screamed at me to run. Told me that this male was a predator and this was a fight I couldn't win, but I wasn't going to hide.

I eyed Kade's sword, which rested on the table where he'd been sharpening it. When my gaze went back to the strange male, excitement had sparked in his black eyes. Like he knew I wanted to grab the sword, and he wanted me to do it. I suppressed my shudder.

"Warrick, what are you doing here?" Locke said, his voice icy.

The male, Warrick, stopped in the middle of the room and opened his arms wide, finally taking his gaze from me to stare at Locke.

"Ah, my son, is that any way to greet your father?"

Father? Now that I was aware of their connection, I saw the resemblance. The angular shape of their faces and lean, muscly builds. Except unlike Locke's, the angles on this male's face were harsher, sharper. He was attractive, but the cruelty shining in his eyes made my stomach roil. I'd thought Locke and the others were monsters when I'd first seen them, but they didn't have the same aura this male had.

"There are worse monsters in this mountain than us." Kade's words floated through my mind. I'd believed him when he'd said it, and the fight with Zacal had already opened my eyes to the truth of it, but it was now, staring at this male, that I truly understood. All the monsters the elders had told us about as we'd grown up. Beings that delighted in tearing apart humans, torturing them just to hear their screams. They did exist.

Sweat slipped between my shoulder blades.

"You know better than to come to my personal rooms," Locke snarled, hatred dripping from his words.

My gaze slid to the sword again, though I knew it would be futile. Could Locke, Kade, and Darian take this monster on? They were powerful, all of them, especially now that I had seen what Kade's wolf could do, but the confidence radiating from this male, Locke's father, gave me pause. If he was like Locke, that meant he had to be the same kind of monster, right? *That means he drinks blood.* I swallowed.

As if he'd heard my words, Warrick sniffed the air and smiled, his eyes landing back on me. He took another step forward, and a growl ripped from Kade's throat. Kade shifted closer to me until my shoulder brushed against his arm. *Oh fuck.*

"There's no need for that," Warrick said with a casual wave of his hand. "I just had to take a look at the new shifter, the last to turn out of this round of humans."

Shifter blood. I remembered the shifter, Lyr, giving Locke vials of her blood. This male had to be part of the Taratun. Did he believe that Lyr's blood had come from me? Something in his eyes told me he didn't.

Locke's gaze didn't falter as he stared at his father. "You've seen her. Now leave."

Warrick's gaze found me again, and I squirmed under his attention. "She certainly is pretty to look at. I can see why you four have decided to keep her away from the others. But you know you're not the only ones who will want their chance to have some fun with her."

Kade snarled, claws beginning to peek from his fingertips, but he didn't move toward the male.

"This one's ours to play with until she joins a house. You have your blood," Locke said, his jaw tight.

Warrick stared at him. "It's a shame she didn't turn into a vampire. It's time you took your place as alpha of the House of Nesarin, son. Fighting for the right to claim her would have been a great show of power. Still, I can see now why you didn't want to hand her over."

At that moment, Asher exited the washroom, a towel wrapped around his waist as he used another to dry his hair. He stopped as he took in the scene. "Oh hell, what am I missin'?" he said, his tone light, though his body tensed.

"Go back to your lab, father," Locke said, ignoring Asher, his voice low and lethal.

Warrick stared at me again, and the eagerness in his eyes had fear coating my tongue. "I look forward to seeing you fight, *shifter*," he said, emphasizing the last word as if it was a joke.

I didn't answer. For once, I was smart enough to keep my mouth shut. We all watched as Warrick glided from the room, closing the iron door behind him.

No one moved for a few heartbeats after he left, but then Locke whirled toward us. "We need to get her to change, and we need to do it now. Warrick's suspicious, and that is *not* a fucking good thing. Raine needs monster blood so we can satisfy his curiosity and get her off his radar."

I didn't bother asking why Locke was so worried about me having his father's attention. If it was concerning him, it was probably better if I didn't know what Warrick did with his curiosities.

"Fear and pain are the best ways to get her to turn. Warrick will take her apart piece by piece if she doesn't change soon. If she dies, we die."

Fear and pain? "Fuck you, asshole," I ground out.

"No," Kade growled. "The trials are over, and there are other ways to elevate a heartbeat. I know you feel the need to protect her like I do."

Locke's chuckle was dark and unkind. "Getting her to change *is* protecting her."

"We knew keeping her here would draw attention," Darian said. "Warrick just wanted to see her for himself."

Rage burned in Locke's eyes, and he smiled, a dark, humorless smile. "Fine. You try your way, but if she hasn't turned in two fucking nights, we're going to have to put her through hell if it gets her to change. Otherwise, she's going to have to compete in the Week of Orash as a human and hope she doesn't get her throat ripped out, or all of us are dead. No one can find out that she's still human."

I glared at him, my hatred for the monsters bubbling to the surface. "Bring it. I *wish* I would turn into monster just so I can get away from your insufferable ass."

Locke's gaze fixed on me, his expression hardening. "Two. Fucking. Nights."

Asher's mouth quirked into a lopsided smile, his violet eyes glowing. "We should get to work, then."

Kade scowled, but he didn't protest.

"Here, Raine my dear, you need this more than I do," Darian said, placing a goblet of wine into my hands.

Locke's grin turned wolfish, and he stepped in front of me, leaning down. "You'd better hope you change quickly, *beautiful*, because once the two nights are up, you're mine."

Mine. I watched his lips as he said the word, and my inner muscles clenched. *His to toy with. To torture.* Well, I was fucking ready. Ready to become a monster and compete in the damn fights. It was my best chance of finding Cara.

"Back the hell up, Locke," Kade growled, folding his arms in front of his chest.

But I just stepped closer to Locke, getting right in his face. Smiling sweetly, I bared my teeth. "I look forward to it, asshole."

TO BE CONTINUED IN BOOK 2:
THE CRIES OF MONSTERS

WANT MORE?

Thank you so much for reading my story! I had such a fun time writing this book, and I really hope you enjoyed it! If you did, please consider leaving a review on Amazon or Goodreads. *The Blood of Monsters* is my debut novel, and unfortunately, if I don't get any reviews I won't be able to sell any books! Reviews help readers discover my books, and I'm so grateful for each one.

For access to exclusive, free *Her Cursed Protectors* bonus material, and to be the first to know about my new releases, join my newsletter via my website *www.miahartson.com*.

HER CURSED PROTECTORS READING ORDER

ABOUT THE AUTHOR

Mia Hartson is an Australian fantasy and paranormal romance author who enjoys writing stories about badass heroines who have multiple partners. (Because the only thing better than one mate is four, right?)

Mia particularly enjoys writing stories with a heavy dose of fantasy, adventure, and spice that keeps you up at night. When she's not writing, Mia's going on adventures with her husband and two girls, singing her heart out, or devouring another book.

For more information about Mia Hartson, her books, and upcoming releases, visit her website www.miahartson.com, Facebook page, Goodreads page or Bookbub.